Travis hadn't  **but talk to H emotional su to friend**

He hadn't counted on how right it felt when he'd instinctively pulled her into his arms to comfort her. Or considered how the look in her eyes as she reached out to him emotionally, at long last, in that distinct woman-man way, would change everything he felt, too.

The boundaries they had painstakingly put in place from the moment she moved in next door had dissolved.

The blinders were off. He saw her as the vital, passionate, loving woman that she was, and the feel of her soft, slender body in his arms sent a charge roaring through him, unlike anything he had ever felt. The tremulous sigh of her breath, the sweetness of her scent and the surrender of her soft lips all combined to further ignite the fire. In just one kiss, one long, sweet, sultry kiss, his whole world turned upside down. Yet never had anything—or anyone—ever felt so right.

Dear Reader,

Christmas inspires us all. There is something about the month of December that encourages people to give of their hearts, their time and their money. For causes, big and small. And to the benefit of friends and family and the people in their lives that they love most of all. But what do we do when a child asks for something we just can't give?

Travis Carson is in that predicament. His daughters, four-and-a-half-year-old Sophie and three-and-a-half-year-old Mia, want a mommy for Christmas, and they expect Santa to bring them one. Travis explains this isn't possible. And because he wants his two little girls to be happy, begins looking for other ways to give them more of the feminine influence they need in their lives.

His best friend and neighbor, Holly Baxter, does not have that problem. Her three-and-a-half-year-old twin sons, Tucker and Tristan, have never really known the father who deserted them shortly after birth, and they don't seem to particularly want a daddy, either. The problem is, their dad is suddenly interested in seeing them again. And Holly isn't sure if this is a gift or a calamity in the making.

Travis and Holly tackle these two problems the same way they approach every other challenge in their single-parent families—together! And before they know it, the Christmas season is bringing them one very wonderful gift, too.

Happy holidays to you and all your loved ones!

Cathy Gillen Thacker

Cathy Gillen Thacker
A MOMMY FOR CHRISTMAS

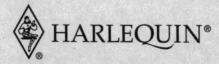

HARLEQUIN®

TORONTO • NEW YORK • LONDON
AMSTERDAM • PARIS • SYDNEY • HAMBURG
STOCKHOLM • ATHENS • TOKYO • MILAN • MADRID
PRAGUE • WARSAW • BUDAPEST • AUCKLAND

Recycling programs
for this product may
not exist in your area.

ISBN-13: 978-0-373-75290-4

A MOMMY FOR CHRISTMAS

www.eHarlequin.com

Printed in U.S.A.

ABOUT THE AUTHOR

Cathy Gillen Thacker is married and a mother of three. She and her husband spent eighteen years in Texas, and now reside in North Carolina. Her mysteries, romantic comedies and heartwarming family stories have made numerous appearances on bestseller lists, but her best reward, she says, is knowing one of her books made someone's day a little brighter. A popular Harlequin author for many years, she loves telling passionate stories with happy endings, and thinks nothing beats a good romance and a hot cup of tea! You can visit Cathy's Web site at www.cathygillenthacker.com for more information on her upcoming and previously published books, recipes and a list of her favorite things.

Books by Cathy Gillen Thacker

HARLEQUIN AMERICAN ROMANCE

Chapter One

Travis Carson did not know what he would do without his next-door neighbor, Holly Baxter. And frankly, he did not ever want to find out. The divorced single mom was always on hand to help him out with his two young daughters. And he did the same for Holly and her twin boys. Their kids attended the same Fort Worth, Texas, preschool. Weekdays, they shared a nanny. Weekends, depending on their individual schedules, a little more.

But most of all, they were friends. And right now he needed a friend with a mother's heart—and accompanying wisdom.

"So what's the problem?" Holly dodged a Christmas piñata and slipped into the booth of the popular Tex-Mex restaurant. She shrugged out of her trendy red wool coat and gloves, then leaned across the table to be heard above the festive strains of "Feliz Navidad," playing in the background. "I assume it has something to do with the kids?"

Travis nodded. He reached into the pocket of the black down vest he wore to ward off the chill at the construction site, and handed over an envelope addressed to the North Pole. "Read it and weep. I did."

Clearly debating whether to take the situation seriously or not, Holly wrinkled her nose, and worked open the seal.

Across the aisle, a tableful of guys in suits were staring admiringly her way. Travis couldn't blame them. At thirty-three, Holly seemed to get more beautiful by the day. Her long golden-brown hair was silky, soft and incredibly glossy. Her skin held the warm glow that came from living in a sunny climate, her five-foot-six frame the sleek, sexy look of a woman who worked out regularly. There was a lot to admire about her lovely girl-next-door features, but it was the genuine trust-worthiness radiating from her wide-set aquamarine eyes that really drew him in. It wasn't just that they were friends—Holly seemed accessible to him in a way no other woman ever had. Which was what made all that ogling from that group of guys all the more annoying. Travis turned and gave them a look.

They got the hint and turned away.

Meanwhile, Holly was transfixed by at the letter she had unfolded. With a curious lift of her elegant brow, she read out loud the words that had haunted him since breakfast.

"Dear Santa,

"We have been very good this year so please bring us the only thing we want this year—a mommy.

"Hugs and kisses, Sophie and Mia."

The bottom and margins of the page were decorated with childish scrawls, stickers and lots of *X*'s and *O*'s.

Holly set the letter down. "Wow." She rummaged in the canvas carryall that served as her handbag. "It's almost as good as the letter Tucker and Tristan dictated to me last night."

Travis kicked back in his seat, enjoying their usual camaraderie. "You can't beat that."

Grinning, she handed over the letter. "Read it and weep."

In the margins of the boys' letter, were crude drawings of airplanes and trucks.

"Dear Santa,
"We want a spaceship big enough to fly away in.
"Love, Tucker and Tristan."

The waitress appeared with a basket of crisp tortilla chips, still hot from the fryer, and some freshly made salsa. She stayed long enough to take their orders, then disappeared.

"So what are you going to do?" Holly asked.

Travis shrugged as the waitress returned promptly with two large glasses of iced tea. "I don't know. I was so taken aback when the girls dictated their letter last night, I didn't know what to say."

"Me, either." Holly sighed.

"When they get it into their head…"

"…that something is possible…" she murmured, continuing his thought.

"It's awfully hard to change their mind," he finished.

"Supposedly it's a stage all three- and four-year-olds go through." Holly munched on a chip. "You know…. where they think they have everything figured out and you can't convince them otherwise."

Silence fell between them.

They locked eyes and exchanged beleaguered grins, both of them knowing how lucky they were to have these kinds of problems—especially at Christmas.

"So what do you want to do?" Holly continued to hold Travis's gaze.

"The usual dinner and a movie?" he offered with a shrug, glad he didn't have to handle the upcoming "explanation" alone.

Holly perked up. "Tonight?"

He nodded. "The sooner we clear this up with the little ones, the better. And we can fit the 'discussion' between the two events."

Holly grinned as the waitress bustled back to their table with two plates of puffy tacos. "Sounds good to me."

THERE WERE TIMES IN every parent's life, Holly Baxter thought, when "backup" was required. Tonight was one of them. Which was why she was so very glad she had Travis Carson to help her face life's problems, big and small.

"What do you mean we have to write letters to Santa?" Travis's daughter, Sophie, demanded with all the indignation a four-and-a-half-year-old spitfire could muster.

"We already wrote them!" her three-year-old sister, Mia, complained.

"And we wrote 'em, too," Holly's son, Tucker, stated in frustration.

"Or at least you wrote down what we said," his three-and-a-half-year-old twin brother, Tristan, concurred.

Holly looked around her kitchen table. The four children looked so much alike, with their blond hair, big blue eyes and cherubic little faces, they could have been siblings. Indeed, during the two years she and Travis had lived side-by-side, the preschoolers had spent so much time together they might as well have been.

Which was what made it so easy to deal with them in a group.

"Your daddy and I know that." Holly took the lead with Travis's tacit encouragement. Emboldened by his sexy, reassuring presence, she continued affably, "But there's a problem with what you all asked Santa to bring you. First of all, boys, they don't make toy space ships big enough for you to climb in, and secondly, toys like that don't fly."

"Well, they should," Tucker grumbled, crossing his arms in front of him.

Tristan stubbornly agreed. "Yeah, how are we supposed to get to outer space if they don't go up in the air?"

Travis gave Holly a look from the other end of her farmhouse-style kitchen table. "They have a point," he mouthed.

She ignored him. If Travis made her giggle, it would be all over.

"Second," she said, even more gently to his little girls, "Santa Claus makes toys at the North Pole, not people, and mommies are people."

Travis nodded as if to say, *Way to go, team!*

"But," Sophie exclaimed, "a mommy is what Mia and I want!"

"Yeah," Mia echoed. "'Cause we don't have one."

Actually, Holly knew all too well that they'd once had a very kind and loving mother. When she had first moved into this house, two-and-a-half years ago,

Travis had just lost his wife. Back then, Diana had been all he talked about. She'd tragically succumbed to a virus that had attacked her heart and killed her in a matter of days.

Eventually, he had come to terms with the suddenness of his late wife's death. But the loss of the woman he had loved more than life had continued to haunt him—just as Holly's unexpected divorce had haunted her.

Eventually, things had gotten better. And now life was pretty much back to normal, Holly thought. With one exception. Neither of them was dating, or intended ever to date again.

"The thing is, girls," Travis interjected quietly, "mommies aren't brought by other people."

"Then how do you get one?" Sophie asked, completely flummoxed.

"Generally, the daddy goes out, and finds a wife. When he marries her, she becomes a mommy," Travis explained.

"Then that's what you should do, Daddy," Mia said, as if it was obvious.

"Yeah," Tucker agreed, waving his arms enthusiastically. "Just go out and find one."

Tristan nodded vigorously. "There's lots of them around. We see them all the time at the preschool."

"Most of those mommies are already married," Travis said.

"Our mom isn't!" Tucker blurted out.

Caught off guard, Holly skipped a breath and felt her pulse ricochet. For a second, Travis looked equally nonplussed. But the moment passed, and Travis took command of the room again.

"What I'm trying to say, kids, is that finding a wife

is a long process and it's not something I have time to do today. I'm very busy downtown."

"Building the Water Tower!" Tucker yelled, excited as always by the thought of bulldozers, cranes and all manner of construction equipment and trucks at the site of Fort Worth's newest mixed-use development project.

"It's called One Trinity River Place," Holly reminded her son gently. And it was quite a coup. Travis and four of his friends each played a role in making the development happen. Grady McCabe had put the deal together. Dan Kingsland was the architect who had designed the three-block-wide, thirty-eight story building overlooking the Trinity River. Travis's company was handling the construction. Jack Gaines's firm was installing all the electronic, satellite and phone systems. And Nate Hutchinson's financial services company was taking up a huge chunk of office space. The rest would be leased out independently. Plus there were retail shops and restaurants going in on the lower floors, and luxury condominiums taking up the top floors. All in all, it was a pretty impressive project. And Holly'd had work there, too. Right now, she was finishing up a mural in one of the restaurants on the ground level.

"Anyway—" Travis looked at all four kids "—the point is it is December 5, and we need to write new letters to Santa, amending what you asked for into something he can actually bring you."

"You know," Holly added for good measure, "something he can actually fit on his sleigh."

"Like new baby dolls," Travis told his daughters.

"Or the bikes with training wheels that you boys have been wanting since last summer," Holly said.

The kids shrugged, their excitement clearly dimmed. "Okay," Sophie said finally.

"That's what we want," Tucker agreed with a disgruntled sigh.

"Can we watch the movie now?" Mia asked. "I want to see what Curious George does tonight!"

"Okay," Travis said. "But just thirty minutes. And then we're going home and getting ready for bed. School tomorrow."

The kids scrambled for places on the *L*-shaped sectional sofa in Holly's family room. They lined up together, various blankets and stuffed animals on their laps. Travis set up the DVD player. A second later, the soothing sounds of the video about the monkey and the man in the yellow hat started.

Travis came back into the kitchen.

From where they were standing, they could see the kids. But the children had their backs to them, and were all focused intently on the story unfolding on the TV screen.

"Well, I guess that went okay," Holly whispered.

He nodded, looking just as uncertain as she felt. Probably because every time the two of them thought they had a situation as tricky as this one handled, it turned out to be not handled, after all. Travis gathered up the pizza boxes and the trash sack. "I'll take this out."

Trying not to think how cozy domestic moments like this felt, Holly forced herself to concentrate on the minutiae of her life instead. "Would you mind getting my mail while you're out there?" she asked. "I think I forgot to bring it in after work."

"No problem. I'll get mine, too." Travis headed out.

Holly loaded the dishwasher.

Travis walked back in, a stack of mail in each hand. "You want to get our trees this weekend?"

Holly nodded. It was something they usually did together. It was easier having another adult helping when trying to select, purchase and wrangle a tree on top of the car in a busy parking lot.

"Saturday morning okay with you?" he asked.

"Sounds perfect." She looked up at him with a smile.

It was funny, Holly mused, how at ease she felt with him. At thirty-six, he bore the perennial tan of someone who spent a great deal of time working outdoors. His dark brown hair was cut in short, casual layers that withstood the elements and the restless movements of his large, capable hands. Like Holly, Travis was a native Texan. He had big ideas, and even bigger goals, and a practical down-to-earth nature she found immensely comforting.

He was also—not that it mattered—a very good-looking man. And quite masculine as well. At six-foot-three-inches tall, he had the big-boned, broad-shouldered build one would expect of a construction worker. A ruggedly chiseled face. Dark chocolate eyes that saw more than he ever said.

He dressed nicely, too. At work, he wore Levi's, canvas shirts, vests and heavy steel-toed boots. The required yellow hard hat. In his off time, the garments he wore were much more expensive. Like the dark brown cashmere sweater he had on tonight, tugged over a T-shirt, with a newer pair of Levi's. His boots were made of really nice, soft brown leather.

He smelled great, too. Like Old Spice and soap, baby shampoo and man...

"Earth to Holly," Travis teased in a low sexy voice, abruptly jerking her back to reality. Startled, she met his grin. "Do you want it or not?" he asked mildly, still trying to hand over the day's mail.

TRAVIS DIDN'T KNOW WHAT was on Holly's mind.

It wasn't like her to lapse into daydreams, unless she was working on a mural. Then she was likely to drift off into that creative place in her heart and mind that brought her so much joy.

But when they were just standing around? Talking? Never.

He supposed it should have been expected, though.

Mrs. Ruley, their shared nanny, could do only so much in the forty hours a week she worked for them. And with both Holly and Travis working full-time, parenting solo, and Christmas coming up faster than a speeding train…

She had a right to be distracted, he thought as he watched her sort through her mail. But not…unhappy. "Holly?" he asked, wondering why her hands were shaking and her face had abruptly gone so pale. "What is it?"

"I don't know," she whispered. She tore open the envelope in her hands, removed the letter and began to read. Her face paled even more. "Oh, no," she cried.

Travis glanced at the kids—they were still entranced by the antics of the monkey and the man in the yellow hat.

His hand around Holly's shoulder, Travis guided her into the mudroom, off the kitchen, where they could talk quietly without being overheard by their brood. "Tell me," he insisted.

"It's a letter from Martin Shield, Cliff's attorney," Holly said, looking even more distraught.

Knowing this did not sound good, Travis folded his arms in front of him. He kept his voice even and matter-of-fact. "And…?"

Holly swallowed. "He wants to meet with me. He says Cliff wants to 'revisit' the matter of custody and visitation of the kids. That we can do it in court, if I wish, but they would prefer to do it less formally, at least initially."

Talk about a kick in the gut! And at Christmas, no less, Travis thought. But then what could you expect from a heartless investment banker who had walked out on Holly when the twins were just barely a month old? "I thought he relinquished all rights at the time of the divorce."

"Cliff ceded full custody to me, and waived his rights to visitation. But he is still the twins' legal father."

"What about child support?"

"With the court's permission, Cliff established very generous trust funds for the twins in lieu of monthly child support, and gave me enough money to buy a house and get back on my feet."

"So it's not about money."

"No. He did way more on that score than he had to do. In that sense, he is a very responsible guy."

"Just not in the personal arena," Travis muttered.

Holly lifted her chin, as if surprised by the emotion in his voice, just as he was. Although maybe he shouldn't have been, Travis thought. He'd come to love Holly's little boys as much as he loved his own children. And he knew Holly felt the same way about his daughters.

He shrugged and followed that with a very sober, searching look. "Sorry, but what kind of bastard leaves a woman with two adorable kids? Asks not to be apprised of their welfare or progress, only to come back over three years later and want to reopen the custody case?"

Holly flashed a wan smile and said finally, in a wry attempt at a joke, "My ex-husband?"

Another silence fell. Every protective instinct Travis had surged to life. "When does the attorney want to see you?"

"As soon as possible." She released a short, impatient breath and continued to hold his eyes like a warrior princess in battle. "He says if I call his office, he'll fit me in."

Travis's frown deepened. "Are you going to do it?"

"What choice do I have?" Holly grumbled, keeping her voice slightly above a whisper. "I mean, I could hire a lawyer, but I don't want to do that—I don't want to go back to court unless I absolutely have to."

Travis couldn't blame her for that. What he knew of divorce court, from those who had been forced to appear there, was not pleasant or pretty. And it would be especially unpleasant at this time of year, which should all be about love and joy, hope and giving. "Want me to go with you?"

Holly nearly sagged with relief. "If you wouldn't mind, I'd really appreciate it," she said, squeezing his hand. "It'll be a whole lot easier to face this crisis with you at my side."

Chapter Two

Travis and Holly sat side by side in the elegant law firm reception area. They were ten minutes early and she was a bundle of nerves, wondering what this was all about.

"So I was thinking…" Travis said quietly, in his attempt to distract her while they waited. His arm nudged hers as he bent his head nearer. "Maybe there is a way to give the kids what they want for Christmas, or pretty close to it."

Jerked out of her reverie, Holly turned to face him. Like her, he was dressed for a business meeting, instead of the construction clothes he normally wore to work. And although she had seen him many times in a suit before, she was struck as always by how handsome and successful he looked.

"What are you talking about?" she blurted, before she could stop herself. "You can't actually be…you're not just going to…!"

"Marry?" Travis shook his head, as if even the idea was ludicrous. "Of course not. But I was thinking we could build your boys a wooden spaceship for the back yard that they could climb in."

"Are you serious?" Holly twisted around fully, her nylon-clad knee nudging his thigh. A tingle went through her at the unexpected contact. Deliberately, she pushed it away.

Oblivious to the awareness suddenly surging inside her, Travis met her eyes. He shrugged his broad shoulders and spoke in a low, mesmerizing tone, "What's the point of owning a construction company if you can't do things to help out your own family, or someone else's?"

True, Holly thought. And it was so like Travis's generous nature to think of it. They needed to be fair in the gift giving, though. She studied his face, zeroing in on the compassion in his dark brown eyes. "What about your girls?"

Travis grinned, pleased she was thinking about his children as much as her own. "Well, obviously, we'd have to build them something for our backyard, too. I was thinking maybe a little cottage they could play house in."

"Ah." Holly smiled. "So although they wouldn't be getting a mommy…"

"…any more than your boys would be able to actually fly to outer space."

"But they would be able to pretend," she concluded.

He nodded. "They're only little once. And maybe this will take the sting out of not having a mom."

And whatever was coming next for her sons, Holly thought pensively.

Travis touched her hand, drawing her back to the conversation. The brief feel of skin on skin was as warmly reassuring as his presence. "So what do you think?" he asked softly.

At the thought of how much joy this would bring to

their offspring, Holly felt a wave of excitement. She found herself suffused with the Christmas spirit once again. "Can we get it done in time?"

He nodded, confident as ever. "Sure. I'll have both items built off-site in the warehouse where a lot of our custom cabinetry is done, and then delivered early on the twenty-fourth."

The first glitch presented itself. "How will we be able to do that without the kids seeing?"

"We'll keep them busy elsewhere until it's dark on Christmas Eve, while the delivery is made. And probably also cover the structures with black construction tarp, to ensure they're obscured from view. We'll take that off while they are sleeping, replace with large ribbons. And when they wake up the next morning we'll give them some time to enjoy what Santa left them under the tree, then take them to the backyard for the big reveal."

"Sounds like a great plan!" Holly exclaimed.

Travis held out his hand for a fist-bump of victory. Holly fist-bumped back.

The receptionist nodded in their direction.

A minute later, they were settled in family law attorney Martin Shield's private office, which was just as old-money-intimidating as the reception area of the venerable Texas law firm.

"I'm glad you agreed to come in," said the distinguished, sixty-something lawyer in the two thousand dollar suit. "Cliff would like to keep this as informal as possible."

Holly's throat was so tight it was all she could do to get the words out. "What exactly does he want?"

"To see the kids."

She had been afraid of that. Determined, however, to play it cool, she held Martin Shield's gaze. "After all this time?" Did Cliff and his attorney not understand how ludicrous—not to mention selfish—this request was?

Cliff's attorney did not bat an eye. "My client is well aware it's been three years, five months and two days since he saw the twins."

Anger surged inside Holly. She had thought the hurt and pain of her ex's betrayal was well behind them. She wanted it to stay that way. "Cliff voluntarily chose not to exercise his right to visit the boys at the time we divorced—over my objections, I might add." Back then, she had been desperate for him to do right by his kids.

"Things have changed. He was making plans to work and live in Europe at the time he divorced you. Now he's in the process of moving back to the United States. His new position is in Connecticut."

Holly wasn't surprised to hear Cliff was on the move again. Frequent transfers were part of the process of climbing the investment banking career ladder. Had the two of them stayed married, she would have been prepared to adapt. Since they hadn't, she was content to stay in Texas and rear her family in the lovely city where she'd grown up. Wanting as much information as possible, she prompted, "So his visit…?"

"Wouldn't be for another fifteen days," the attorney stated. "Handled any way you want."

Despite her effort to play it cool, Holly tensed. "And if I don't agree?" she asked in a brittle voice.

The esteemed attorney was ready to play hardball.

"Clifford Baxter wants to see his sons. Legally, he has every right to do so."

Holly said nothing. She was so furious at her ex's mixture of presumption and disregard for their children's feelings in all this that she didn't trust herself to speak.

Abruptly, Mr. Shield became conciliatory. "My client is just asking for a couple of hours one afternoon. He wants to see his children, get an inkling of the little men they've become."

Holly knew if she fought this, they'd end up in court. The result would be the same. Cliff did have every legal right to see his children. It was only a question of how, where and when. Making the process difficult for him would only make it tough on her kids. They had been disregarded enough already. "All right," she conceded at last. "Two weeks from Saturday, Cliff can see the children in my home, under my supervision."

"I will be there also," Travis interjected.

Holly looked at him. Feeling as if she could drown in his empathetic eyes, knowing it would be all too easy to depend on his inherent kindness even more than she already did, she nodded her assent.

The lawyer's brow furrowed. "And your relationship with Ms. Baxter is what exactly?" he prodded.

"A friend," Travis replied, then reached over to squeeze her hand. "A very *good* friend."

"WANT TO TALK ABOUT IT?" Travis asked, after ten minutes had passed and Holly had yet to say a word about what had gone on. Instead, she appeared deep in thought. A little sad. And a lot worried.

"I don't think so." She forced a smile as he parked

next to the Carson Construction trailer that served as his private on-site office.

Travis got out of the Expedition and watched as she did the same. Damn, but she looked good today, in that feisty "I can handle anything that comes at me" way....

Not that he should be noticing, given the fact that their relationship was strictly platonic, he reminded himself sternly.

She strode purposefully to her minivan, released the latch and removed a garment bag from the cargo area. Her knee-length skirt and high heels seemed out of place in the dusty, rough-paved parking area.

He tore his eyes from her spectacular legs and visually instructed all the other workers in the area to do the same. "Need a place to change clothes?" he asked casually.

"If you wouldn't mind." She ran a hand down the skirt of her sexy, cardinal-red business suit. "I can't really paint in this and I've got to finish the mural at the restaurant. I promised them it would be done today."

He moved ahead of her to open the door. She took the two concrete steps into the mobile office that served as his command center. In the front room was a desk, drafting table, phone and several computers.

In the middle was a long table and chairs. Behind that, a private bath, complete with shower and a closet where he kept extra clothing.

"You can change in the conference room," Travis said. "I'll stand guard to make sure no one comes in."

"Thanks." She shut the door behind her.

Travis shrugged out of his suit coat, sat down at his desk, pulled up his e-mails. Made a few phone calls. Accepted a few more.

And still no Holly.

Wondering what was keeping her, he got up and went to the door. Rapped lightly. "Holly?"

There was no answer. Feeling his heartbeat picking up, he rapped again and spoke louder. "Everything okay in there?" Again, no answer.

So there was only one thing he could do.

HOLLY DIDN'T KNOW WHAT was wrong with her. She could *not* stop crying. And she had been trying for nearly ten minutes now.

Grabbing a hand full of Kleenex from the box on the bathroom counter, she opened the door and was startled to see Travis standing on the other side. Tall and indomitable, he sent her a brief, telling look that spoke volumes about his inherently understanding nature. The emotion still building inside her took another giant leap. "I thought this might happen," he said gruffly.

The next thing she knew his arms were around her. Her head was on his chest, and the sobs she'd been holding back came out in harsh, ugly sounds that had been years in the making. And still they came—on and on and on, until she thought she would die of embarrassment.

Through it all, Travis simply held her, moving one hand over her spine, threading the other through her hair, the action as comforting as his presence.

Until eventually she did stop crying.

And feeling all the more mortified, she stepped out of his arms, only to bump her hip into the bathroom counter.

She started in surprise and caught a glimpse of herself in the mirror.

Red puffy eyes, redder nose and quivering chin.

The distressing sight of her weakness was enough to make her tear up again. "Lovely," she said with disgust. She knew she couldn't afford to let her defenses down for one instant when it came to ensuring her children's well-being. Like it or not, she was all they had.

And as for this sudden interest of Cliff's—every maternal instinct within her said it wouldn't last. But it would certainly cause havoc in the meantime….

Travis put his hands on her shoulders and turned her to face the mirror again. "Yes," he said simply, clearly meaning it, "you are lovely—even now. And you're also distraught. And I think it's high time we talked."

Holly preferred to handle her problems all by herself, but she also knew she couldn't shoulder such a pressing burden without talking to someone. And since Travis was her best friend, and most frequent companion, he was the likely choice.

He took her by the hand and led her back into the conference room, and to a chair. He pulled up another, so they were sitting across from each other, and waited patiently.

Glad she had Travis to lean on, she said finally, "I'm afraid Cliff has realized what a mistake he made when we divorced, in voluntarily ceding full custody to me."

"Why did he do that?" Travis asked gently, covering her hands with his.

Holly shrugged, aware she never talked about this. It was just too humiliating. She leaned toward Travis's warm and strength, and turned her palms upward, so their fingers were loosely entwined. "Cliff said he realized he was not cut out to be a father, and he wasn't going to pretend to be interested in the kids when he just wasn't."

Incredulity mixed with the concern on Travis's face. He tightened his grip. "How old were they?"

Holly sighed, remembering that awful time in her life. "Tucker and Tristan were four weeks old the day Cliff told me he wanted a divorce, and walked out. They were four months old when the divorce was final."

Travis released his hold on her, sat back. "That's fast."

She shrugged and kept her voice matter-of-fact. "He wanted out. He went to the Dominican Republic."

Travis searched her face, finally settling on her eyes. "And since then?" he asked quietly. "Any other flickers of interest from him?"

"No. I haven't heard a word. He's never expressed the slightest interest, and given how he felt about Tucker and Tristan—" Holly felt her chin begin to quiver again, as she focused on the deficit of love her sons had received from their biological father "—I was relieved. They're such great kids."

"They deserved a hell of a lot better," Travis agreed brusquely.

"Yes." Holly thought about what this could to do to her happy-go-lucky kids, if it was handled the wrong way. "They do deserve a whole lot better!" She suddenly pushed herself out of the chair and began to pace. "Which makes it all the more bewildering. I don't understand why he's doing this."

Travis rose, too, and caught up with her. "Maybe he realizes he made a mistake in letting you-all go."

Holly scoffed in response. "I don't think so." She shut her eyes, aware she was near another onslaught of tears. "Oh, Travis," she whispered miserably. "What if he wants to take the kids away from me?"

Travis embraced her again. "He's not going to do that." He silenced her protest with gruff certainty. "I'm not going to let him."

Gratitude mingled with the overwrought emotion inside her. Holly held him tighter, needing him—his steady male presence and enduring friendship—as never before. And that was when it happened. She saw him the way she would have seen him, when she'd first moved into the house next to him, had she not been so overwhelmed with responsibility and mired in grief over her failed marriage. In that instant, she saw him not as the single dad next door, but as the wonderfully virile, exciting, incredibly principled and loving man he was. Desire swept through her, more potent than any spark she had ever felt before.

At that moment, something wonderful and mysterious shifted in his eyes, too. And then suddenly his mouth was on hers, and the unexpected embrace robbed her of breath and the will to resist.

Holly had never imagined what it would be like to stand wrapped in Travis's strong arms, her body flush against the hardness of his. Now that it was happening, now that he was actually kissing her, it seemed unreal. And yet utterly amazing and satisfying in a way she never could have fathomed.

For starters, Travis tasted so good, in a way that was unique to him. His lips were soft and tender, the sweep of his tongue evocative and warm, as he brought her back to life, reminding her of all that had been missing for years now in her celibate existence.

And, unbeknownst to her, she evoked the same feeling in Travis.

When he had walked into the conference room, he hadn't meant to do anything but give Holly the emotional support she needed, friend to friend. He knew she was upset, and deservedly so. He hadn't expected to find her crying as if her heart would break, hadn't imagined how simultaneously devastated and protective he would feel as he came to her rescue. He hadn't counted on how right it felt when he instinctively pulled her into his arms to comfort her. Or considered how the aching vulnerability in her eyes as she reached out to him would change everything he felt, too.

The boundaries they had painstakingly put in place from the moment she'd moved in next door had instantly dissolved.

The blinders were off. He saw her as the vital, passionate, loving woman she was, and the feel of her soft, slender body in his arms sent a charge roaring through him unlike anything he had ever felt. Her tremulous sigh, the sweetness of her scent, the surrender of her soft lips all combined to further fan the fire. With just one kiss—long, sweet and sultry—his whole world turned upside down. Yet never had anything—or anyone—ever felt so right.

Which was why he had to stop it now, before any further boundaries were crossed, and they compromised their current relationship. Shaken to the core, he lifted his head and forced himself to let Holly go. Trembling, she stepped back, too, regret in her eyes. Without another word, she picked up her garment bag and purse. Head down, eyes averted, she rushed for the door.

And Travis knew he had moved way too fast, and in doing so, might just have put everything he held near and dear in jeopardy.

"ARE WE GOING TO TALK about this?" a familiar male voice asked five hours later.

A tingle went down Holly's spine. She kept right on painting the last little bit of detail of the piazza mural on the wall of the Italian restaurant. "I don't see why we should."

Travis strolled nearer, looking incredibly masterful in his work clothes and yellow hard hat. "Because if we don't, that kiss will always be the elephant in the room. And I for one don't like living in a zoo," he drawled.

His lame attempt at a joke eased the tension between them somewhat, as he had to have known it would. Holly sighed and put down her paintbrush. She flashed him a sassy smile she couldn't really begin to feel, considering the mess they were in. "You really want to know what I think?" she asked softly.

Looking as if he had all the time in the world, Travis perched on one of the sawhorses. "I really do," he replied, an emotion she could not clearly define in his dark brown eyes.

"Okay." She wiped her hands on the rag tucked into the belt of her jeans, feeling her cheeks flush at the distinctly male satisfaction in his smile. "My defenses were down because I was clearly out of my mind this morning with worry."

He paused, clearly caught off guard by her revelation.

Holly pushed on, determined to be honest. "I don't blame you for kissing me—given the way I was acting. Like I wanted you to ride to the rescue."

Another loaded silence fell between them.

Holly paused to lick her suddenly dry lips. She didn't

know how he could look so cool, calm and collected, when she felt so frazzled.

She stepped closer so they were toe to toe, then forced herself to go on with the speech she had been mentally preparing all afternoon. "I can see why you would have thought…"

She watched as he rubbed a hand across his closely shaved jaw.

"Hell, for a moment, I thought…maybe…" She pushed away the memory of that mind-numbing kiss. Ignoring his slow, sexy smile, she swallowed around the sudden lump in her throat and continued sternly, "But you know as well as I do that it would be wrong for us to go down that path. Especially this time of year."

He narrowed his eyes. "What do the holidays have to do with this?"

Holly pivoted and moved back to the sawhorse opposite him. "You know how a lot of people get all excited and go out and buy puppies at Christmas to give as gifts?"

He nodded, skeptically.

"They think they want a puppy and are prepared for one—and at first it really is great having one around. But before you know it, the puppy gets a little older and…"

"Poops on the floor?" He wryly guessed at where she was going with this.

Holly rolled her eyes, aware he had just broken her train of thought, which was perhaps his purpose. "All silliness aside, you know what I mean," she persisted, determined to make her point. "What seems like a great idea when you're all caught up in the spirit of the holidays often loses its luster after December 25."

"I would buy that theory." He gave her a long, steady look. "Except for one thing."

Determined to hold her ground, she folded her arms in front of her. "And what's that?"

Triumph radiated in his smile. "You weren't enthralled with the Christmas spirit at the time we kissed."

We kissed. A thrill went through her at just the memory… She lifted her chin and put a practical spin on their disturbing lapse in judgment. "My being worried that my ex is going to ruin the holidays with his machinations is more or less the same thing. Whatever Cliff is trying to do put me in a highly emotional state! I turned to you without thinking about the impact this could have on our lives."

He lifted a discerning brow. "And now that you are thinking about consequences?" he challenged.

She let her glance drop to his broad shoulders and sinewy arms. "I don't want to lose our friendship or complicate our lives unnecessarily, because you know as well as I do that *sex changes everything.*"

"So you want me to forget kissing you again."

Was that disappointment in his low tone? And in her heart? Could she afford to fall victim to these feelings? Especially when she knew romance was based on the illusion of perfection, and that the illusion could never last, when confronted with the wear and tear of everyday living and familiarity.

Once again, Holly let her common sense take over. "Yes, I do," she reiterated. "For both our sakes."

Travis was quiet a long time. His expression remained maddeningly inscrutable. Finally, he stood and said. "The last thing I want is to upset you or give you any more trouble than you have at this moment. So whatever you want, whatever you need—" he paused and looked into her eyes "—let me know. And I will be there for you. No questions asked. No holds barred."

Chapter Three

Once a week, the principal players in One Trinity River Place met for lunch. The meeting always started with business matters that needed to be handled, and ended with more personal conversation among the five long-time friends.

"I see why you're concerned," Grady McCabe told Travis over lunch the next day.

"We all are," Dan Kingsland agreed, cutting into a steak.

"None of us want to see Holly hurt," Jack Gaines said, with typical overprotectiveness where women were concerned.

"And it certainly sounds like that's what her ex has up his sleeve," Nate Hutchinson agreed.

Travis forked up some salmon. He trusted the guys to be objective, in a way he couldn't be in this particular situation. "So none of you think I'm overreacting here?" *Letting my emotions get in the way of sound judgment and common sense?*

"It's not that Holly needs protecting, per se,"

Grady—the first of the four single dads in the group to marry again—murmured.

Dan, who had also recently found the love of his life, nodded in agreement. "Ninety-nine percent of the time Holly can handle herself just fine."

"It's the one percent we worry about," Jack said.

"And I have to wonder," Nate continued, with the cynicism of the only bachelor in the group, "what has happened to make Cliff Baxter suddenly change his mind about seeing the kids."

Grady frowned. "What exactly do you know about the dude?" Grady asked, getting down to brass tacks.

"Not a lot." Travis looked around the cozy wood-paneled dining room, which was decorated in exclusive-men's-club style. "Holly never wanted to talk about him."

"And now?" Jack prodded.

He thought back to the way Holly had cried yesterday—as if her heart would break. How she had nestled against him as he'd held her. And the way she had kissed him back...as if nothing mattered at that moment, except the passion they'd found with one another.

Grady tilted his head. "Has something changed between the two of you?"

Travis worked to keep a poker face. It wasn't easy. Part of him wanted to shout to the world how mind-blowing that steamy embrace had been. The more private part of him knew this was no one's business but his and Holly's. His desire to protect her in every way intensified. "What do you mean?" he asked casually.

The guys exchanged looks. Eventually, Nate said, "We always figured...you and Holly are so close...."

"Hell, you're practically living together," Grady stated.

Jack added somewhat awkwardly, "We just assumed sooner or later the two of you would start dating or something."

After that spectacular kiss, Travis had hoped that would be the case. Until Holly set him straight about her own expectations. "I don't think that's in the cards," he said carefully.

"If you say so." Dan looked unconvinced.

"Holly and I are friends," Travis said firmly. And he didn't want anything interfering with that—even their one ill-timed, incredibly sensual kiss. Reluctantly, he forced himself to put the memory of their passionate moment aside and concentrate on the problem at hand. "I want to help her be prepared for whatever is coming with her ex-husband."

"Then you're going to have to do your homework," Nate said. "And find out everything you can about Cliff Baxter and what might be motivating him."

TRAVIS CANCELED AN AFTERNOON meeting and set up one with the private investigator who handled all the background checks and preemployment screening for his workers.

When she arrived, he ushered Laura Tillman into his on-site trailer. The statuesque redhead was one of the best in the business. If there was something to be found, he had confidence she would get it.

Laura listened quietly and took notes on everything he told her.

"How soon do you want the information?" she asked in a brisk, businesslike tone.

Travis rocked back in his chair, beginning to relax a

bit, now that he was taking a more proactive approach to the situation. "As soon as possible. Definitely before he comes to Fort Worth to see the kids."

"Does Holly know you're doing this?"

Guilt filtered through Travis. "No. And I'd prefer she didn't find out."

Laura fell silent, considering all the angles. "This could backfire on you, you know," she warned.

Travis turned his attention to the Christmas pictures Sophie and Mia had colored for him at pre-school. Next to those were a couple from Tucker and Tristan. "I know."

"But?"

"I want her to be prepared. And this isn't the kind of thing she would do on her own."

"Whereas you have no scruples," Laura teased.

He had guilt, all right. Plenty of it. It wasn't like him to go behind Holly's back. He wished he didn't have to do it now. "In this case, the end justifies the means," he stated.

Laura put her notebook into her carryall briefcase. She paused to study him. "You really care about Holly, don't you?" she mused.

Warmth filtered through him at the acknowledgment. "Of course." He forced himself to be practical. "We're friends."

Laura lifted a skeptical brow.

"Just friends," Travis repeated, as much to himself as to the P.I.

"Mmm-hmm." Laura grinned, still not buying his denial. She stood, all business once again. "I'll call you as soon as I figure out what's going on."

"Thanks." Travis circled around his desk.

He and Laura were nearly to the exit when the door opened, and Holly walked in. "Oh!"

Travis thought he saw a fleeting glimpse of jealousy in her eyes. Aware that he had jumped to conclusions about the depth of her interest in him the day before, and been wrong, he pushed the tantalizing notion away.

She smiled and tucked a strand of long, golden-brown hair behind her ear. "I didn't know you were busy." Her tone was casual.

Trying not to notice how great she looked in her loose blue chambray painting shirt, snug-fitting white T-shirt and jeans, Travis welcomed her in with a matter-of-fact smile. "It's okay. We're finished." *Thank God.*

"Hey, Holly," Laura said, smiling as well.

To Travis's relief, the private investigator looked as innocent as the day was long as she headed for the exit.

"Hey, Laura," Holly said, just as nonchalantly.

The two women exchanged easy glances and then Laura slipped out, closing the door behind her.

Travis drank in the alluring, feminine fragrance of Holly's perfume as she neared. Putting a damper on his reaction, he forced himself to focus on the reason for her unexpected appearance. He searched her aqua-marine eyes. "Everything okay?"

She nodded, but he could tell from the excessive ease in her manner that she was putting on an act for his benefit.

Her next smile was even more maddeningly aloof. "I just wanted to see if we were still on for Christmas tree shopping tomorrow," she said.

Travis pushed aside his remorse, at having gone behind Holly's back to protect her and the kids. He focused on the weekend, and the fun they usually had together, instead, reminded of what a good team they made. "Absolutely. The girls and I are looking forward to it."

Holly continued looking at him, her expression becoming inscrutable. "Okay," she said finally, backing out with a shrug. "I'll see you then."

THE WORST HAD HAPPENED, Holly thought to herself as she drove home that evening after work. Travis had kissed her—and she had kissed him back—and now he was acting weird around her, when all she wanted to do was move forward as if nothing had happened.

Fortunately, she had the evening to pull herself together.

She did two loads of laundry, changed the sheets on her bed. Then spent the night alternately worrying about what Cliff was really up to and obsessing over the kiss that should never have happened.

She awakened early, dreaming about Travis's soft, sure lips, her pillow clasped tightly in her arms.

Telling herself to get a grip, she rose and headed for the shower.

She had just walked into the kitchen to prepare breakfast for the boys when the phone rang. Caller ID said it was the man who'd never been far from her thoughts. Smiling despite her worries, she picked up the receiver.

"Help," Travis said, his husky baritone a balm to her ravaged nerves. He whispered into the phone. "I've got a blueberry muffin emergency."

He sounded so distressed, Holly couldn't help but chuckle. "A what?"

"Just come over here."

Finally, it seemed, they were back to normal. "I'll get the boys and be right there," Holly promised.

Tucker and Tristan were delighted to be going next door, so it was no problem to get their jackets on and hustle right on over. They slipped through the back gate of Travis's picturesque cottage-style home.

Like hers and most of the others in the neighborhood, it was approximately three thousand square feet, and was filled with overstuffed sofas and chairs upholstered in kid-friendly fabrics, plus sturdy wood furniture. The rear of the house had sunlight streaming in the many windows, lighting up the large open area that was kitchen, breakfast room and family room combined. Next to the carpeted play area, where Mia and Sophie were busy with a big box of building blocks, an armoire held a flat-screen television. Instead of a coffee table, there was a long, rectangular ottoman that opened up for storage. The large fireplace took up most of one wall, and matched the collage of charcoal and light gray stone on the outside of the house.

Tucker and Tristan said a distracted hi to Travis as they struggled out of their jackets, then made a beeline for the girls.

"So what's going on?" Holly asked.

Travis looked great in a soft evergreen pullover and jeans. Wool socks and handsome suede moccasins covered his feet. He waved her to the kitchen, nicely out-fitted with white cabinets, speckled black granite countertops and pale gray walls. He turned on the oven light and opened the door slightly so she could peer in.

"Are you cooking biscuits or muffins?" Holly murmured, noting the specks of blueberries poking through the pale, rubbery looking dough.

"Muffins!" Travis said in frustration. "The girls wanted them, and we didn't have any boxed mix. But we had blueberries, so I got out the cookbook and decided to make 'em from scratch."

Holly checked out the recipe, which looked fine. She looked at the ingredients spread out on the counter, spotting a familiar yellow box, but no can. "Did you use baking soda or baking powder?" she asked.

Travis hesitated.

Realizing how rarely he looked uncertain about anything, she smiled.

"There's a difference?" he asked.

Oh, yeah. Holly moved closer and kept her voice low as she instructed, "Show me what you used."

He handed her the baking soda.

She peered into his cupboards, which were as familiar as her own, and pulled out a small red can. "This is baking powder. This is the leavening agent you put in cakes and muffins to make them rise."

"Oh." He went to back to check the muffins, which were looking sicker and paler and more rubbery by the moment. "So now what?" He scowled, considering, then turned back to face her, his arm nudging hers in the process.

Warmth filtered through her at the brief, accidental contact.

While she savored the sensation, Travis concentrated on the mistake he had made and the dilemma at hand. "Do you think it would help if we sprinkled some baking powder on top of the muffins or stirred some in?"

Holly shook her head, sorry to deliver the bad news. "Not at this point in the baking process."

"Daddy, we're hungry!" Sophie declared.

"Are the muffins ready?" Mia asked, looking

hopeful, hungry and excited all at the same time. "Tucker and Tristan want some muffins, too!"

He shrugged. "Well…?"

Holly took the oven mitt from him, reached past him, hit the off button on the control panel and took the muffin pan from the oven. "Get your shoes on, kids!" she instructed.

Travis read her mind and went to get jackets for all. "We're going *out* for breakfast today!" he announced cheerfully.

FORTY-FIVE MINUTES LATER, Holly and Travis were seated at a hard plastic table, enjoying their premium coffees and apple Danish pastries, while the kids—who had downed their own breakfasts in record time—climbed on the indoor playground. "You see, for every culinary disaster there's a silver lining," Holly teased.

Travis exhaled in frustration, still a little embarrassed by the mistake that had brought them here. He shook his head wryly. "I really thought I had it this time."

She reached over and gave him a friendly pat on the arm. "You almost did," she told him with a smile.

Travis shot her a level look. "If I built buildings the way I follow recipes," he acknowledged dryly, "I'd be in big trouble."

Holly held up a slender hand, cutting off his self-deprecating remarks. "You're a very capable man." She paused and wrinkled her nose at him playfully. "You just can't cook anything that doesn't come out of a box or a jar or a plastic bag."

Travis waved at the kids, who were peeking through a mesh safety barrier at them, then turned back to Holly.

"You do it with aplomb. So do a lot of other single parents—men included. My friend Jack, for instance, is an excellent cook. Jack's daughter loves his cooking, the more gourmet the better."

Holly's eyes sparkled as she met his gaze. She leveled him with a look of her own. "First of all, it's not a competition, between you or me and you and Jack or anyone else, okay? You parent in your own way, just as I do, and furthermore—" a self-conscious pink crept into her cheeks "—you're a fantastic dad."

Looking at her determined expression, Travis could believe it. Still, he didn't like falling short in any category, and that went double when it came to anything pertaining to his kids. "Maybe I should take some cooking lessons," he murmured.

"You really want to do that?" Holly looked surprised.

A little irked that in some ways she knew so little about him, and what made him tick, Travis tapped the center of his chest and countered, "What? Are you worried I'll flunk out of the class or something?"

"No. Of course not. I just didn't think you'd have time for something like that right now, with the holidays and the Trinity River Place project. And isn't there something else you fellows are bidding on?"

Travis nodded. "A steering committee was just formed by some of the city's leading philanthropists. They want to build a new opera hall if the funds can be raised, and we want to be ready if the project comes to fruition." He paused. "And speaking of business, what's on your schedule for the next two weeks, now that you've finished the restaurant mural?"

"Next week I'm doing murals for three exam rooms

in a new pediatrician's office. And a nursery mural for Grady and Alexis's new baby after that, although I'm still waiting for Alexis to okay the design. We're supposed to meet at her office next week."

"You sound busy, too."

Seemingly as reluctant to break up the cozy tête-à-tête as he was, Holly glanced at her watch. "Which is why we better get a move on if we want to get both our Christmas trees up and decorated today."

SIX HOURS LATER, THE trees were up and twinkling in both their family rooms. Dinner and dishes were over. It was breaking up the four kids that was proving to be the problem.

"I don't want to go back to our house, Daddy," Sophie said with a pout.

"Me, either." Mia stamped her foot. "I want to stay here with Tucker and Tristan and Holly."

"You all need baths and pajamas," Holly decreed.

"Why can't they take their baths here?" Tucker asked.

"Yeah, they've done it before, plenty of times," Tristan argued.

Holly looked at Travis. He, too, seemed to be wondering if this was a battle worth fighting. Suddenly, wordlessly, they were in agreement. "Okay," he told the four kids. "You all can have your baths here, but they're going to be quick ones tonight."

"And then we get to watch *A Charlie Brown Christmas* together like you promised!" Sophie reminded him.

They *had* promised, Holly recalled. Hours ago. When they'd had no idea how long it would actually take to do all they had done.

Travis lifted his hands in surrender. A promise was a promise….

"Okay." Holly relented, too. She and Travis exchanged empathetic looks before she continued. "And then everyone is going to go to sleep in their own beds."

"Are we going to get new Christmas pajamas this year?" Tucker asked, once all four kids were back downstairs again, getting settled on the sectional sofa.

"Yeah, ones that match!" Tristan said.

"Of course," Holly replied. That was one wish that was easily granted.

Travis looked at her with a question in his dark eyes. "It's a family tradition," she explained. "The kids get new pajamas on Christmas Eve and wear them to open their presents Christmas morning."

"Well, we want to do that, too," Mia said.

"Yeah, and we want ours to look just like Tucker's and Tristan's," Sophie added.

Holly had no earthly idea what to say to that. For one thing, boys' and girls' pajamas were usually quite different in color and style. And Travis's daughters favored pink!

"Can we?" all four kids said at once. "Please…can we?"

Yet again, Holly looked at Travis. And once more, he took the lead. "Sure," he said, turning on the TV. The video started, and all four kids fell silent.

"Do you ever think our families are a little too integrated?" Holly asked, when the two of them had retired to the kitchen.

Travis watched her spoon fragrant decaf French roast

coffee into a paper filter. Like their kids, he found himself wishing the evening would never end.

Aware that Holly had paused, waiting for an answer, he said adamantly, "No. I don't think our lives are too enmeshed." In fact, there were nights—long, lonely evenings like the night before, when they each did their own thing with their own kids—when he wished they were more entwined.

Holly set the coffee on to brew, then turned around. She lounged against the edge of the granite counter, her hands braced on either side of her, and searched his face. "You never wonder what will happen if one of us moves away?"

Travis moved so they were a foot apart, and his arms folded in front of him. "I'm not going anywhere." He thought of Cliff's sudden reappearance in her and the twins' lives. Uncertainty made him tense. "Are you?"

Her expression said that was a ridiculous question. "Well, no…"

Travis shrugged and held his ground. "Then it isn't an issue," he said flatly, wondering when things had gotten so personal between the two of them.

A pulse throbbed in Holly's throat. "It could be if you started dating someone."

"I'm not interested in remarrying. You know that." Or at least, Travis amended silently, he hadn't been until he'd kissed her. That had opened up such a realm of possibilities he no longer knew what the future held. Except for one thing. The woman next door. His best friend. "Are you?" he persisted.

"No," Holly answered, just as quickly and resolutely. Her soft lips compressed stubbornly. "I decided long ago that's not in the cards for me, either."

"Then what's the problem?" Travis asked softly, wondering what suddenly had her so on edge.

Holly winced and rubbed her temples. "I don't know."

Travis was pretty sure she did know—but didn't feel comfortable sharing all her concerns with him.

Looking as if she wished the conversation had never started, Holly shrugged off her melancholy mood and moved away from him toward the family room, where the TV was flickering. Her tender smile turned into a quiet laugh and a shake of her head. She put a finger to her lips, then motioned for him to join her.

He walked over. From where they stood, they could see over the top of the sectional sofa. The video had barely gotten started, but all four kids were sound asleep, lying snuggled up to each other like a pile of snoozing puppies.

Travis chuckled, too. "I'll have to carry them home and put them to bed," he said.

Holly tipped her face up to his. Once again, she looked so content. His heart filled with admiration and something else—something sweet and satisfying—he wasn't sure he was quite ready to identify.

She propped her hands on her hips, obviously as reluctant to spend another Saturday night alone as he was. "Want to have a cup of decaf first?"

He liked the spark coming back into her aquamarine eyes, the generous, easygoing attitude she exhibited whenever they hung out together. A wave of tenderness swept through him, as potent as it was unexpected. "Sure."

She fell into step beside him as they moved toward the kitchen, both of them reveling in the peace and quiet after a very noisy, tumultuous, busy day. She reached the coffeemaker, then paused to look into his eyes. "By the way, thank you for everything. It was a great day," she told him softly. "A really great day."

Happiness warmed his soul. "I thought so, too," he admitted. And it could be even better if they said to heck with what had been till now, and followed their instincts.

Holly started to speak. Travis didn't know what she was about to say—all he knew for sure was that it was going to have to wait.

HOLLY SAW THE KISS coming and knew she could have stopped it. All she had to do was put a hand to his chest, keeping distance between them, or turn her head and step back. She did none of those things. Instead, for once in her life, she followed her deepest impulses, which led her straight into Travis's arms.

When his mouth descended, she wreathed her arms about his neck and went up on tiptoe to meet his lips. Before she knew it, she was lost in a storm of heat and need, tenderness and yearning. He caught her upper lip between the two of his, rubbing it softly, then did the same to her lower lip. Holly responded. Together, they found all the ways their lips could fit together, torment and caress. Until that wasn't enough, and his tongue slipped inside her mouth, to stroke and play with hers. Warmth swept through her; tingles centered in her middle and spread outward. Lower still, she felt the pressure of his need against her. And the desire welling up inside her, unchecked.

"I thought we weren't going to do this," she reminded him, trembling.

"So did I." He smiled down at her with lazy familiarity. "We thought wrong."

Travis wrapped his arms around her again, hauled her close and kissed her once more, really kissed her. And this time, when the embrace finally ended, Holly didn't want to list all the reasons why they shouldn't be giving in to recklessness and pure, unadulterated physical need.

It was Christmas.

This was a gift.

They really didn't need to know more.

Except…

A self-conscious flush moved from her neck to her cheeks. "I want you to promise me that if we go down this road, embark on something…casual…that fits our situation…we'll just go with it, without worrying about all the implications."

His eyes turned serious and he shifted her closer once again. "Sounds good."

Panicking a little at the fierceness of her emotions, she pushed him away, drew in a shuddering breath. "But if for some reason it doesn't work out…" Acutely aware how much was on the line here, she gripped the hard muscles of his biceps urgently. "I can't lose you." Her voice caught. "I can't lose all this…and if our going down this path brings up even the possibility of that… then I can't."

Nor could he.

Travis held her eyes with his. Sifting his hands through her hair, he vowed, "Nothing will come between us—I promise you that."

Chapter Four

A blue norther roared in overnight, whipping up the wind and dropping the temperature twenty degrees in a matter of hours.

The abrupt change in weather mirrored Holly's mood. She'd gone to bed still feeling the glow of Travis's kisses, and their decision to let whatever happened along those lines happen.

She had awakened wondering if she'd made the right decision, after all. She had never been the kind of person who acted impulsively or had a fling, never had sex with a friend. So her inclination to do so now was disconcerting, to say the least.

She knew the decision to add passion to the platonic friendship she and Travis shared felt "right" at the moment. Especially since neither of them was interested in dating or remarrying. But how would it feel in two days, two months or two years? She couldn't help but wonder. Would they one day regret this? Want more? Less? If they eventually had to backtrack, would doing so hurt their friendship, or make their relationship so awkward they would never feel the same in each other's presence? If so, how would they explain that to the kids?

She was still wrestling with her ambivalence when her phone rang early Sunday afternoon.

"I need to go to the pharmacy to pick up some prescription allergy medicine the pediatrician called in for Sophie," Travis told her over the phone, sounding so harried her heart went out to him. "I was going to take the girls with me, but I don't think that's an option."

In other words, Holly thought, it was Meltdown City over there.

"Any chance you might be able to come over for fifteen minutes and spot me?"

Glad to be able to help lighten his load the way he often had hers, she said, "Sure. Let me round up the boys and I'll be right there."

Tucker and Tristan were delighted by the chance to see "their best friends in the whole wide world." They promptly got into their jackets and raced across the frigid yards to get to Travis's front door, where they punched the doorbell with childish vigor.

Holly winced, imagining what that sounded like inside. "I think that's enough, boys."

Travis opened the door with an amused grin. Three-year-old Mia had hold of one of his legs. Tinsel decorated her blond curls. She peeked around to greet the boys, squinting her eyes and wrinkling her nose. They did the same back, then all three burst into riotous giggles and raced off.

"I'm coloring!" Mia shouted over her shoulder, as the tinsel she'd been wearing as a crown went every which way. "Want to color, too?"

"Sure!" the twins enthused in unison.

Travis stepped back to let Holly pass, and bent to pick up a few errant strands of silver. "Come on in."

She grabbed a couple strands, too, and handed them over to him, to be returned to the tree. "Where's Sophie?" It was unusual for the four-year-old, self-proclaimed leader of the Baxter-Carson posse not to appear at the door, too.

Abruptly, the light went out of his eyes. Travis pressed his lips together in parental concern. "On the sofa in the family room," he said quietly.

Knowing something was up, Holly stopped midstride and curved a hand around Travis's biceps to halt his progress. That was all it took to remind her of the kisses they'd shared, and her reaction to them. Forcing herself to ignore the jolt of attraction zipping through her, she concentrated on the problem at hand.

Her back to the breakfast room table, where the three younger kids were madly coloring, laughing and talking all at once, she asked with the bluntness of a close and trusted friend, "What's going on? I mean, aside from the fact Sophie's under the weather?"

Travis held Holly's glance, seeming relieved that she was there. "I'm not sure what's going on with Sophie. She's been cranky and glum all day. Part of it is her allergies—I know she's not feeling good." He frowned in concern. "But there's something more bothering her, too."

It was frequently easier, Holly knew, for children to unburden themselves to someone other than a parent, whom they were often trying to protect. "Want me to see if I can figure out what it is?"

"That would be great," he told her gratefully. He strode

over to the sofa, where Sophie lay curled up on the throw pillows, her favorite baby doll in her arms. He hunkered down beside her and patted her shoulder consolingly. "Holly's here, sweetheart. So I'm going to take off."

Sophie's lower lip curled out and she demanded pitifully, "I want to go to bed, Daddy."

"All right. I'll get you tucked in…."

"No! I want Holly to do it." Sophie coughed until she could barely catch her breath. Her nose ran and her eyes watered. The little girl was clearly miserable, and Holly's heart went out to her. "That darn cedar pollen," Holly said sympathetically. "It gets you every year." And it had been really stirred up by the winds the night before.

"I know." Sophie sniffed again and lifted her hands, signaling that she wanted to be carried.

Travis hoisted her into his strong arms, and she dropped her head in the curve of his neck. "I want Holly to carry me," she protested weakly.

Travis shook his head. "You're too heavy, sweetheart."

"I'll be right behind you," Holly promised. Sophie coughed again, harder this time, her congestion evident. "You still have a vaporizer?"

"Yep." Travis strode down the hall and deposited his daughter on the white trundle bed in her room. He stepped back to let Holly take over. "I'll get it out for you."

She drew back the pink-and-white covers, and Sophie climbed beneath them. Holly grabbed a tissue from the container on the bedside table and gently wiped the moisture from beneath the child's nose.

"You always make me feel better." Sophie flashed a wan smile.

"Being around you always makes me feel better,

too," she said with a burst of maternal love. She tucked the covers around the little girl.

Travis came back in carrying the vaporizer, he set it atop the bureau and plugged it in. The muted sound of the motor and a whoosh of cool moist air immediately followed. "That's going to help you feel better," he promised. Then he looked at Sophie. "Anything else you want me to get you while I'm at the drugstore?"

"No." His daughter snuggled next to Holly and held her hand tightly. "I have a *mommy* to make me feel better. That's all I need, Daddy."

SOPHIE'S WORDS WERE LIKE a blow to Travis's heart, bringing up every anxiety he had ever had about parenting his two little girls on his own. From the look in her eyes, Holly seemed equally taken aback, unsure what to say. Because he had no clue, either, Travis simply nodded in understanding and headed off for the pharmacy.

When he returned twenty minutes later, medicine in hand, the younger kids were still coloring, laughing and talking. Holly was upstairs with Sophie, propped against the headboard, reading to his daughter.

And while his little girl still looked physically miserable, emotionally she was much better off. Feeling a bit frustrated that he hadn't been able to reassure her himself, Travis measured the medicine in the little plastic cup, stood by while she drank it, then handed her the juice box chaser that would kill the yucky taste of the antihistamine decongestant mix.

"Can Holly spend the night with us?" Sophie asked.

"No, honey, I can't," she said, keeping her glance

averted from his. "But I can stay a little longer this afternoon if it's okay with your daddy."

"It's great with me," he agreed, letting his tone tell Holly how much he appreciated her being there, since she still wouldn't look him in the eye. Probably because she was afraid she'd give too much away if she did. "I'll be downstairs if you need me," he said.

Both of them nodded. Judging by the silence that followed, he would barely be missed.

A half hour later, Holly came downstairs and said hello to the kids, who were now congregated in the family room, busily rearranging all the kid-safe decorations on the lower limbs of the Christmas tree.

She moseyed over to the kitchen, where Travis was sitting. "You doing okay?" she asked softly.

Nodding, he gestured to the laptop computer in front of him. "I've been ordering Christmas gifts online."

Holly's eyes lit up with comically exaggerated excitement. She pulled a stool next to him, propped her chin on her hand. "Anything for me?"

"We doing what we did last year? One gift each, with a ten-dollar limit?"

Which had translated to gag gifts that related back to the kids—a reusable ice pack in an elastic-bandage sleeve from him, and a giant box of cartoon character Band-aids from her.

She studied him now, an inscrutable expression on her pretty face. "Is that what you want?"

Much seemed to be hinging on his answer. Wary of making a mistake that would take them off the track they were on, Travis pretended the kind of indecision he rarely felt. "I don't know. Let me think about it," he drawled.

But Holly wouldn't let it go, any more than she had been able to keep from kissing him back the night before.

"Meaning what? You want us to *stop* giving gifts to each other?" she teased.

Other direction, Travis thought, knowing that, once again, much hinged on his answer. Since he rarely lost when he went after what he wanted, he looked her square in the eye. "Actually…I'm thinking maybe it's time we started giving each other gifts on a par with what we really mean to each other."

"So what am I supposed to make from a comment like that?" Holly asked Alexis Graham McCabe the next afternoon. A matchmaker by trade, Alexis was also Grady McCabe's wife, and one of Holly's best female friends.

Alexis lifted a hand. "First—did you agree to up the ante on the gifts?"

"Well, yes. It would have seemed wrong not to, given all he and I and our kids have come to mean to each other," Holly admitted self-consciously. Not that she had a clue what she was going to give Travis, or he her. "Now back to my question. What am I supposed to infer from him making a move like that?" she demanded, still feeling off-kilter from the numerous changes Travis kept throwing her way. Big or little, it didn't seem to matter—every alteration left her feeling as if she was no longer in charge of the direction of her life. She hadn't felt that way since she had been married to Cliff, and it wasn't a comfortable feeling, now or then.

"What do you want to infer from it?" Alexis asked with a wry grin, from behind her sleek glass-and-chrome desk at Foreverlove.com.

"Well, I don't know!" Too restless to sit, Holly paced around the room.

Alexis stood, too, and moved over to join her at the window overlooking downtown Fort Worth. "Sure you do," she said gently.

Holly turned back to her friend. These days, Alexis had it all. A stepdaughter who adored her, a husband who loved her more than life, a thriving career and a baby on the way.

"What exactly is your relationship with Travis?" Alexis walked to the festive jar of peppermint bark on her console and wordlessly offered Holly the yuletide treat.

She shook her head. "No, thanks."

"You seem to be more than casual friends," Alexis noted.

"We're best friends."

"And…?" Alexis munched on a piece of candy, waiting.

Holly blushed as she thought about the kisses she and Travis had shared. "What are you fishing for?" she snapped, shocked and embarrassed by how much the embraces had meant to her.

Alexis straightened a stack of holiday cards from satisfied clients, then settled on the arm of a love seat, assessing Holly with a professional eye. "What do you want your relationship with Travis to be? Do you want to be romantically involved with him?"

Holly flushed even more as an image popped into her head of her and Travis in bed, locked in each other's arms. "Romance is a tricky thing to sustain." She had failed miserably at it before.

"Not when true love is involved. And if you want my professional opinion, I think you and Travis have

enough chemistry to light up every Christmas tree in the
Lone Star State!"

Holly suspected that, too. "The thing is, he was really
in love with Diana, his late wife. To the point that when
I first met him I didn't know if he would ever get over
losing her." Holly didn't want to compete with that.

Alexis understood. "It took me a long time to grieve
the loss of my late husband, too. And while I'll always
have a special place for Scott in my heart, eventually I
knew it was time to move on, to really start living again.
And that's when I met Grady, and everything changed
in the most wonderful and amazing ways." She paused.
"I know it's different for you. You're divorced. But
getting over that kind of loss takes grieving, too.
Looking at you today, I think you've finally done that."

Holly had. She tilted her head, attempting to lighten
the mood. "Are you trying to fix me up?"

Alexis grinned and adjusted the star atop the tabletop
Christmas tree in her office. "Are you in the market for
a matchmaker?"

"No," Holly murmured. *I already know the man I
want.* The question was, did she have the guts to go after
him? And what if she risked everything, only to fail, just
as she had before, when she was married to Cliff?

Alexis continued studying her. "If I may offer a word
of advice…"

Holly could use an objective opinion from a friend.
And if there was anything Alexis was an expert on, it
was man-woman relationships. "Please do."

"I know you're hesitant to rock the boat. I can't blame
you. Your life, in many ways, is perfect right now."

And lacking in others, Holly thought, recalling how

she'd felt when Travis kissed her, and the restlessness she'd felt ever since.

"But in my experience people in situations like these get closer, or they drift apart. I've never seen two people sustain a platonic relationship at the level of intimacy you and Travis have, without one of you eventually wanting more and taking it to the next level, or getting frustrated if it doesn't happen," Alexis warned. "And when that occurs, well, it usually signals the end of the friendship as they knew it."

Disappointment spiraled through Holly. "So you're saying?" she asked, feeling anxious again.

"I think this is one of the times when you need to consider which direction you really want your life to go. And then act accordingly."

"HOW DID YOUR MEETING with Alexis go?" Travis asked later that afternoon, when Holly went over to his home to collect her two kids.

Their shared nanny, Mrs. Ruley, waved on the way out the door.

"Great," Holly said. Alexis had given her a lot to think about. Plus things had gone well from a business perspective. "She really liked my proposed mural of the characters from the Beatrix Potter books for their nursery."

"I'm not surprised. The preliminary sketches you showed me yesterday were really sweet. Just like the artist."

Were they flirting? Holly blushed. Apparently, they were.

"And speaking of sketches…" Travis grabbed hold

of her wrist. He eyed the kids, who were all entranced in building a play village on the family room floor. Then he tugged her wordlessly into the walk-in pantry. "I need sketches, too," he whispered as they cleared the portal.

"Of what?" Holly playfully whispered back.

He mocked her with a look, clearly impatient for them to get on the same page. "The playhouse and the spaceship," he explained. "I talked to Dan. He's going to have one of his architectural interns draw up the plans tomorrow, so my crew can start building it immediately. First, we have to know what they're supposed to look like. So…can you do it this evening after the kids are in bed, and get them to me in supersecret fashion?"

She grinned. *Supersecret, indeed.* "Yes, of course," she said dryly.

He hadn't needed to tug her into the walk-in pantry to ask her that! But now that he had… Holly gazed up at him and her lips parted. His mouth lowered at approximately the same time two tiny hands clamped around their legs.

Holly looked down and saw Tucker standing between them, with a curious expression on his face. "Whatcha two doing?" he asked.

"Talking," Travis replied innocently.

"About what?" Tristan demanded.

"About secret Christmas things!" Travis confessed, hoisting both little boys in his arms.

"I want to know about the Christmas secrets!" Sophie raced to join them, with Mia on her heels.

"Me, too!" her sister cried.

"Well," Travis said with great drama, "Holly and I

were thinking that *maybe…*" he paused, and Holly could tell he was doing this on the fly, trying to come up with something good.

"You kids should give each other Christmas presents this year!"

"Hurrah! Presents!" they all shouted.

"And that means we're all going to have to do some Christmas shopping this weekend," Holly continued.

"Sounds good to me," Travis said. He winked at her and leaned down to whisper in her ear, "Great save!"

Yet another example of what a good team they made.

THAT EVENING, LONG AFTER the kids were sound asleep in their beds, Travis and Holly met in the side yard between their two houses. Up and down the pastoral suburban street, exterior lights twinkled and decorations added a festive air. Overhead, the black velvet sky was lit up with hundreds of stars and a beautiful crescent moon. The scent of wood smoke and the faint aroma of baking sugar cookies filled the air.

Holly shivered in the light coat she had thrown on, while Travis studied by flashlight the sketches she had done. "I really like all the fancy stuff on the exterior of the playhouse," he said. "And this spaceship is going to be phenomenal."

"I thought we'd furnish the playhouse with a table and chairs and maybe a little kitchen set. And have bench seats and a control panel in the spaceship. Maybe a steering wheel or two in front of the Plexiglas window, so they can really feel they're flying the ship."

Travis shook his head in admiration. "I knew you would come up with something great."

She flushed, basking in his praise. "You're the one who's going to be building it."

He shrugged. "With help from some of the apprentices who work for me."

Holly knew he'd be hands-on in making sure they got what they wanted for their kids. "In any case, it's going to be a Christmas to remember." It was still two weeks away and the children were already so excited!

"Yes. It is."

Travis carefully slid the sketches into the Carson Construction folder he had brought with him, and took them over to his SUV. When he returned, he appreciatively inhaled the aroma wafting on the air. "We are definitely going to have to bake some cookies soon," he said.

Holly laughed. Those cookies did smell good. "Maybe this weekend."

"Speaking of which…" Travis smiled. "Grady and Alexis are having the holiday potluck for our social group at their house, and they would really like you and the boys to come. During the party, Grady's daughter, Savannah, is hosting a 'movie and game night' for the other little kids— and also a sleepover for any child who wants to stay on." He searched Holly's eyes. "So what do you say? Saturday? Four o'clock? All you have to do is show up with a casserole or something. We could carpool if you like."

"Actually, Alexis already mentioned it, earlier today."

"And…?"

"I told her the kids and I would love to come," she replied.

Travis grinned, as aware as she was that with sleeping children inside their homes, they really needed to get back. "Too bad we can't just run away and do something completely reckless and irresponsible right now," he whispered.

Indeed. "Ah, well," Holly murmured, wishing she could give in to impulse and kiss him again. "Duty calls." She marshaled her common sense and, with one last, wistful look, started to turn away.

"You're right," Travis agreed. "But before it does…" He encircled her wrist with his fingers and tugged her toward him. When she collided with his chest, he wrapped one arm around her waist and threaded his other hand through her hair. "How about this?"

The next thing she knew, his lips were on hers—and once again she was reminded of how much she had been missing ever since the twins were born. Friendship and teamwork could satisfy her only so far. She knew continuing down this road would be risky, but he tasted and felt so good, so undeniably hot and male. Desire made her tremble inside and she thrilled at the sensation of his deep, mesmerizing kisses. Warmth swept through her and still they kissed, until her pulse hammered in her ears and she could hardly catch her breath.

She was throbbing when they slowly drew apart at last. Holly looked up at Travis as a car turned into the driveway across the street, ending their private moment.

"I never felt this much like a teenager when I was a teenager," she confessed, wishing their make-out session didn't have to end.

"Me, either," Travis agreed, looking as if he wanted nothing more than to take her to bed and keep her there. "But I like it," he murmured quietly but honestly.

Holly grinned, figuring this once that she would say exactly what was on her mind. "So do I."

Chapter Five

Holly strode into the preschool Monday afternoon, still perplexed about the request that she stop by as soon as possible to discuss the morning's activities. It was three o'clock and all the students had gone home. A film crew from the local television station was set up in the gymnasium, near the stage that had been decorated to look like Santa's home at the North Pole. It looked like they were wrapping up.

She turned to search out the twins' teacher, Ms. Garland, and ran smack-dab into Travis. Seeing him here was both a relief and a worry. He narrowed his eyes in concern, looking just as confused as she felt. "Did the school call you, too?"

Holly nodded. She stepped close enough so they could confer without being overheard. "Ms. Garland said they had something they wanted me to see."

"Same here." Travis frowned and ran the flat of his hand across his smoothly shaved jaw. "I got a call from Sophie's teacher as well as Mia's."

As if on cue, both the teachers in question joined them. The preschool director and Delilah Porter, a stunning blonde features reporter they both recognized from her constant appearances on the local news, was there, too. "Why don't you step into my office?" the director asked everyone.

She led the way, the reporter following close behind. Travis stepped back to let Holly precede him into the room. The educators followed.

After introductions were made, the director turned to Travis and Holly. "You both signed a release allowing your children to be filmed for a human interest story on kids and the holidays."

Holly and Travis nodded in acknowledgment.

It was obvious the features reporter was supremely excited about what had transpired—to the point she could hardly contain herself. "The students were filmed singing the songs from their December music program," she said, "and then interviewed about what they thought they would be doing for the holidays. Interestingly enough, Tucker, Tristan, Mia and Sophie all had the same goal."

She switched on the portable TV monitor. "We figured you would want to see this yourself." Delilah fast-forwarded through her taped intro to the news segment, and the singing. Then returned to normal speed when she reached the portion featuring the kids gathered in a semicircle, sitting cross-legged on the floor. "Santa Claus" was seated in the middle. The sweetly familiar voice of Travis's daughter filled the room as she spoke to the bearded, snowy-haired gentleman in the fur-trimmed red suit.

"We were going to ask you to get us a mommy for Christmas," Sophie was explaining to Santa, with such grown-up seriousness it nearly brought tears to Holly's eyes. "But then Daddy said that you couldn't do that. He has to find a *wife* first, and get *married* to her, and *then* we'll get a mommy."

Oh, no, Holly thought as the others chuckled uneasily.

"Yeah," Mia agreed, on screen.

"And we're going to help them," Tucker promised, gung ho as usual.

Tristan nodded, equally exuberant. "Because Sophie and Mia are our very bestest friends."

"Only we don't know where to look for a wife," Sophie told the deadpan Santa.

"So can you tell us?" Mia persisted. "So Daddy can have a wife and we can have a mommy?"

Santa stroked his beard. "Well, no, actually, I can't," he replied thoughtfully. "But maybe this is something you should discuss with your daddy again."

"They can't do that," Tucker interjected.

Tristan held up his palms on either side of his head. "*Then* it wouldn't be a *surprise!*"

Mia agreed. "And Christmas presents are s'posed to be a su'prise."

Delilah Porter stopped the footage. "I'll take it from here," she informed the faculty. The director and two teachers filed out.

"Tell me the news station isn't going to run that," Travis said, mortified.

"Of course we are!" she exclaimed. "It's the kind of story that touches the heart and is perfect for Christmas." She leaned forward eagerly. "I'd like the two of you to be part of it, too."

Holly held up her hand, already backing away. "Uh, no. And for the record, I'm against running that little bit with our kids, too."

"Lucky for me, then, isn't it," the reporter said, "that you've both signed a release, giving the station permission to air any and all footage."

Silence fell.

"But, that said, we still have time to let you respond to what your little girls asked Santa," Delilah Porter told Travis. She leaned out the door and waved to a cameraman, then turned back to him. "You're a widower, right?"

"If you have any conscience," Travis told the stunning blonde, "you'll do the right thing and cut my kids from the piece." He exited the room.

Holly stayed. "Travis is right. Running that story as is would hurt the kids."

Delilah peered out the door at Travis's tall, masculine figure as he stalked out of the building. "Or it could help that sexy single dad find a wife just in time for Christmas," she speculated.

Holly supposed that was true. If all the single women in Fort Worth thought a catch like Travis was ready to marry again, it wouldn't matter if he was or not. They'd be beating a path to his door, attempting to be The One for him. Holly hated to think what havoc that would bring to both their lives.

Delilah eyed her closely. "You're his next-door neighbor, right?"

Holly grasped her handbag tightly. "What does that have to do with anything?" she asked, wishing she'd left with Travis.

The cameraman was at the door, blocking her exit, ready to film.

Holly held up a hand. "I haven't signed a release," she reminded him sternly.

The reporter motioned for her crew to back off. "Your kids seem awfully close," she noted.

Holly shrugged. "We live next to each other and they play together all the time," she stated casually.

Delilah gave her a look meant to inspire confidence. "Would you like to be interviewed? Perhaps shed some light on this situation?"

Holly shook her head. "No. I wouldn't." And following Travis's lead, she exited the room.

BY THE TIME HOLLY REACHED the parking lot, Travis's SUV was gone. Which was funny. She would have figured he'd wait for her. But then, maybe he hadn't wanted to risk another run-in with Delilah Porter.

Holly got in her car and put the key in the ignition.

Her cell phone rang. She smiled at the name flashing on the caller ID and picked up. There was no need for preliminaries. "Where are you?" she demanded.

"Where Delilah Porter can't find me." Travis's husky voice rippled through her.

Holly relaxed when she realized some of his usual good humor had returned.

"Meet me at the Shipley Do-Nuts one mile south of the preschool?" Travis asked.

"Right away," she promised, glad they were going to have the chance to figure this out together. It always helped when she didn't feel alone.

Travis had parked around back, so Holly did, too. Her

pulse rising in anticipation, she walked into the small, heavenly smelling shop. He was already seated, with two cups of hot coffee and two of their fresh-baked potato-flour doughnuts on the table in front of him.

"You read my mind," Holly said, as he passed her a doughnut and coffee.

Frosted vanilla-nut was her favorite type of yeast doughnut from the famed Texas bakery—as he well knew, since they often took the kids here for a special weekend treat.

Travis had opted for a chocolate frosted yeast doughnut. "I figured we should indulge ourselves, given what we just heard. Although it's not as bad for you as it is for me," he acknowledged with a rueful twist of his oh-so-kissable lips.

Holly stirred two creams and one sugar into her coffee. Briskly, she brought him up to date. "For the record, I asked Delilah Porter not to run the piece."

"And?" Briefly, hope shone in his eyes.

Holly sighed. "She refused, and tried to interview me instead."

Travis kicked back in his chair, his knee brushing hers under the table as he tried to get his large body situated comfortably in a too-small space. "And just when I thought this Christmas season could not get any more difficult," he lamented.

Sensing he needed comforting, as any friend in this situation would, Holly reached across the table and took his hand. The warmth of his palm felt as good as a cozy blanket on a frigid winter evening. "Look," she said, as she gazed into his eyes. "I know this is embarrassing...."

His fingers melded to hers. "You think?"

Holly responded with the levelheaded approach to the problem he needed to hear. "But the segment will air, and people will probably chuckle at the naïveté of your little girls and feel empathy for their desire for a mommy. And then they'll go back to their own holiday plans, and that will be that."

Travis sighed. "I know the embarrassment will pass. My kids' Christmas wish may not. Obviously, they still really want a mommy."

He turned his hand over, so their palms were pressed together. The feel of that was oddly intimate. The contact reminded Holly of the kisses they'd shared, and the intensely physical longing that welled deep inside her whenever they were alone lately. Again she forced herself to deny what she wanted, and instead, gave him what he needed—comfort and advice.

"And one day you'll fall in love and marry again and they'll have one. In the meantime," Holly counseled softly, "they have Mrs. Ruley."

Travis studied her, still making no effort to release her hand. "And you."

"And me," Holly murmured.

Silence fell between them. Holly looked deep into his eyes, wishing for the first time that the two of them hadn't met at such a tumultuous time in their lives, become such devoted friends. She wished there was still some mystery left, that they could test the growing physical chemistry between them in a way that was as romantic, unexpected and complication-free as they both deserved. But to go down that road—to risk the passion not working out— might be to risk their friendship. And where would either of them be without that? Holly wondered.

Abruptly, Travis seemed to be thinking the same thing.

He flashed a wan smile and disengaged his hand from hers. "You really think we'll both fall in love and marry again?" he asked her finally, meeting her gaze once again.

Holly hadn't thought so—until now. "Yes," she said, meaning it with all her heart. Her little boys might not be asking for one, but they needed a father, and would one day realize that, too. Whether that would be Cliff— because he had finally come to his senses and realized what he had given up—or someone else, was a question for another day.

"But in the interim," she continued, appreciating Travis's steady male presence, "we still have each other."

Contentment lit his eyes. "You're right about that," he said, picking up his cup.

"So in regards to the reporter?" Holly asked.

Travis downed the rest of his coffee and vowed, "Delilah Porter has already got all the story she's going to get from me."

UNFORTUNATELY, TRAVIS SOON realized, wanting a situation to be over did not necessarily make it end.

The TV piece on his and Holly's four kids' determination to find him a wife for Christmas, so his little girls would have a mommy, hit a chord with viewers. The station ran the piece again and again, and posted it on their Web site for viewers who still couldn't get enough.

Reporter Delilah Porter dug into his background and learned about his wife's tragic death, his thriving business and his devotion to not only his little girls, but also to his attractive next-door neighbor's twin sons.

And she did a story on all that. It didn't matter that Ms. Porter did not have their cooperation; she managed to get photos of all parties involved and cute anecdotes about what wonderful single-parent families they were from multiple other sources. That story, too, was aired many times.

Other reporters—not to be outdone—called repeatedly, asking him to comment. As did one of the New York City based morning news programs.

Travis refused all invitations. As did Holly.

On Wednesday, the Fort Worth and Dallas newspapers asked him to comment. Again, he refused…so they ran their own versions of the story, and received an abundance of reader mail.

On Thursday, the local radio stations got into the act. Thinking it might end the cacophony if he said something, Travis finally consented to a brief five-minute interview with a local radio host. Travis explained his situation and reiterated his belief that his children would let this idea of theirs go, if everyone else did the same. Listeners were enthralled.

Fan mail started pouring in.

Women were calling the office, calling his home, leaving messages, offering to solve his problems…and fulfill his little girls' dreams.

And that was nothing compared to the nonstop ribbing he got from the construction crews at One Trinity River Place….

By the time they all arrived at Grady and Alexis McCabe's for the annual potluck slash kid pajama party early Saturday evening, Travis had had enough unwanted attention to last him a lifetime.

"Do you want to be the one to tell him?" Grady asked his wife, after the four preschoolers were settled in with the other kids in attendance. "Or should I?"

Knowing Alexis worked for a professional match-making agency made Travis almost afraid to ask what he was talking about.

"Foreverlove.com has been getting a lot of calls wanting to know if you're one of our clients, and if not, how come," Alexis said with a smile.

Holly stiffened. Although why that should bother her, Travis didn't know. She had laughed off all the mail he was getting. As well as the occasional letter she received, advising her either to snag him for herself, or be a real friend and get out of the way, so he could find a suitable mate.

"But not to worry, Travis." Alexis held up a reassuring palm. "I told them you're not in the market just yet."

This observation made Holly even tenser, Travis noted.

He watched her retreat into the adjacent family room, where the kids were all gathered around the big-screen TV, giggling at a movie about a little boy who had a Christmas calamity every five seconds, it seemed. She paused to talk to Dan's eldest daughter, seventeen-year-old Ava.

Travis turned to his four best male friends, all of whom were lounging around the kitchen, helping themselves to the collection of dips, chips, and hot and cold appetizers set out. "If anyone has any idea how I can get my daughters and Holly's twins off this tangent, I'd like to hear it."

"Actually get married again?" Dan suggested, as the pregnant Emily Stayton took her place beside him.

Although the two hadn't set a wedding date yet,

everyone in the group knew it wouldn't be long before they did.

"Travis doesn't need to get married," the devoted bachelor in the group, Nate Hutchinson, said. He angled his head at Holly. "Travis has all he needs in his best pal, living right next door, without the complications of wedded bliss."

Except sex, Travis thought. Ironically, he was so busy working and taking care of the kids he hadn't had time to miss it—until he and Holly kissed. Now it was all he could think about.

Alexis gave her husband a pointed look. "I think you fellas should back off," she told Grady.

"Travis should know how many eligible women want to be matched with him," Grady retorted.

"Unless some lady already has his heart," Jack observed in amusement.

Not again, Travis thought. *"Et tu, Brute?"* he said.

Jack shrugged. "Just calling it like I see it." He grinned.

Holly ambled back in.

Travis gave everyone a look advising them to find something else to discuss, lest she be upset again. They complied, and the rest of the evening passed pleasantly.

At eleven, the evening was winding down. Dan's two teenagers had left several hours before and all the younger kids were sleeping soundly in kid-size bedrolls on the family room floor.

Correctly reading Holly's and Jack's hesitation about leaving their kids for the night, Grady grinned. "They're going to be fine, you know."

"You can come over and get them as soon as they

wake up," Dan said, with the experience of a father who had much older kids, and had been through all this before.

Travis knew what Holly was thinking—that their kids had never slept over at anyone else's home before, except each other's.

"They'll be fine," Alexis reiterated. "Grady and I are going to sleep on the pullout sofa. If anyone wakes up in the middle of the night, you'll be the first to know."

Reluctantly, Holly tore herself away. Feeling oddly bereft himself, Travis followed her out to the car. "A portent of the future, hmm?" he murmured.

"In my case—if Cliff prevails—maybe sooner than either of us realize," Holly said glumly.

Travis knew that suddenly dealing with the prospect of an emerging custody fight with her ex-husband had to be incredibly hard for Holly. Struggling for the right words, he saw her safely inside, then circled around the SUV and climbed behind the wheel. "Have you heard anything more from your ex?" he finally asked.

Holly shook her head. "Just a note from his attorney, advising me that Cliff plans to bring some Christmas gifts for the kids, when he sees them."

Travis studied the sober lines of her mouth. "And you think that's a bad sign?"

Holly clamped her arms in front of her as if warding off a sudden chill. "I don't know what it means," she replied carefully. "I guess I'll find out next week."

Travis turned up the temperature on the automatic thermostat. As a new blast of warmer air shot out of the vents, Holly shifted toward him, the shoulder harness pressed into the soft, womanly curves of her breast.

Travis schooled himself not to notice the fact that she was chilled, even as he felt the blood pool low in his body.

Holly raked her teeth across her bottom lip. "Do you think I should be worried?" she asked.

Travis had an uneasy feeling, too, which was why he'd gone outside his own comfort zone, where his and Holly's relationship was concerned, and surreptitiously asked private investigator Laura Tillman to find out what she could about the situation. Travis knew self-centered guys like Cliff usually didn't act unless there was something in it for them. The question was what. If Cliff had gotten an ego boost from having sired two sons, Travis figured that Holly's ex would have come around long before now. He could want Holly back... and Travis could certainly understand that. What he couldn't fathom was how Cliff had ever let a woman as spectacular as Holly go in the first place. If she had been *his* wife... But she wasn't—she was his best friend—and he needed to remember that.

Aware the P.I. had promised to get back to him with results before this weekend was over, Travis turned into his driveway, cut the motor and reached over to squeeze Holly's hand. He wished he could be honest with her now, but until there was something definitive to report, he was not going to worry Holly further. She had enough on her plate as it was just dealing with Christmas and the children.

"I'm not going to let anything bad happen to you or the kids," Travis promised firmly. "And you can count on that."

HOLLY DID COUNT ON Travis's protection—maybe too much, she thought. The bond between them was so deep and complex she didn't ever want to let their "partner-ship" end. Yet she was well aware, should Travis ever fall in love again, their close bond would most likely have to be severed to keep from interfering in his new marriage. And while she wished him every happiness possible, the prospect of her having to give up their friendship was daunting, to say the least.

What would she ever do without him?

Would she ever have to find out?

Holly decided if she were to have a single Christmas wish come true, she'd want to never be without Travis.

Because being near him made everything seem so much better....

With a bemused smile splitting his handsome face, Travis remarked, "In the meantime, we should probably savor this moment." Having successfully recaptured her full attention, he teased warmly, "It's not often we have an evening sans kids."

Almost never, Holly thought. And never with the two of them alone. Was it her imagination, or was their neighborhood more decked out than ever this year? Holly wondered, looking around, at the dazzling array of festive lights and yuletide decorations covering the houses and sprucing up the lawns.

All she knew for certain was that it was a magical moment, on what suddenly seemed like a very magical night. A night that had started out with some rollicking family fun now felt remarkably like a date.

"Want to come in for a nightcap?" Travis asked, as they got out of his SUV.

A nightcap, Holly repeated silently to herself, as he circled around the car to her side. She chuckled and shook her head in bemusement. She winked at him salaciously, to add to the joke. "That almost sounds like you're trying to seduce me."

"Would I have a shot at it if I was?" he responded casually.

Holly turned toward him, saw the cool, purposeful intent in his eyes, and caught her breath. The next thing she knew his tall body had caged her against the closed passenger door. Despite the brisk December air, she felt the heat emanating from him faster as their bodies merged.

Tingles surged through her, pooling in her lower abdomen, tautening her nipples. Damn, but she wanted him. So very much… Had wanted him for longer than she cared to admit. "I thought we were smart enough not to do this," she whispered, aware they were standing on a precipice that could lead to great joy or utter disaster.

Travis threaded his fingers through her hair. "At one point, so did I," he admitted huskily.

But they weren't, Holly thought, as he brought her closer still and his mouth found hers once again. His lips were cold, in contrast to the heat of his tongue. He tasted like coffee, mint and man, and Holly felt herself surge to life. Maybe it was the season. Maybe it was the fact she was feeling a little jealous and a lot threatened by all the attention Travis was getting, thanks to their kids' determination to find him a wife. All she knew was that she didn't want anyone else to have him, didn't want anyone else doing this. Not now, not ever, she thought, as the kiss went on and on.

Travis drew back as a car passed by, its headlights sweeping across the yard, catching them in full clinch. "We should go inside."

Holly knew what would happen if they did. She also knew how long it had been since she had been this close to anyone. How much she wanted him. Wordlessly, she tucked her hand in his.

Travis led her up the walk. They moved onto the porch, then through the front door and into the front hall.

The downstairs was lit selectively, the lights on the tree glimmering. The fragrant scent of evergreen added to the magic feel of Christmas hovering in the air. Travis shrugged off his coat, drew hers away from her, too. And then she was back in his arms, going up on tiptoe, threading her fingers through his hair, guiding his mouth back down to hers.

The kiss was a melding of heat and need. Yearning spiraled through her as he moved his hands tenderly over her spine, across her shoulders, down her arms to her wrists and fingertips. And still they kissed and kissed, the feel of his mouth on hers filling her with the kind of love she had wanted all her life. For the first time, Holly felt treasured in that special man-woman way. If she hadn't known better, she would have thought she had finally found the soul mate she had been desperately searching for.

But they were *friends* and she was terrified that getting swept up in this impossible fantasy could shatter the foundation of their real-life relationship.

So how come she couldn't muster the strength to turn him away?

"I want to do this right," Travis murmured, oblivious to the conflict swirling through her. Framing her face with his hands, he murmured, "May I take you upstairs to my bed?"

Holly trembled with a mixture of anticipation and nerves. Leave it to Travis to give her a choice every step of the way. "After a kiss like that," she whispered back recklessly. "I'd be crushed if you didn't."

Surveying her with distinctly masculine satisfaction, he tucked one arm beneath her knees, the other behind her shoulders, and swung her off her feet. Her heart pounding, Holly held on to his broad shoulders. "I'm not sure this is necessary," she laughed.

He grinned back, clearly not about to let her go. "Why not let me be the judge of that?" he asked huskily. Her excitement escalated. Down the hall they went, to the master bedroom. It was as neat as hers. A refuge of masculinity in the sea of toys and videos and little girl belongings that permeated the rest of the house.

His eyes glowing with a sensual, determined light, Travis set her down beside the king-size bed with the charcoal-gray comforter and coordinating dove-gray sheets. The world narrowed to just the two of them as his hands slipped playfully beneath the hem of her black wool skirt, smoothing over her black tights, along the inside of her thighs. Aware that she had waited a lifetime to feel like this, Holly shuddered as he found her through her clothes.

"Travis." Her arms encircled his neck and she threaded her fingers through his hair. With a groan of desire, he captured her lips with his. She kissed him back thoroughly, loving the way his tongue stroked hers, once and then again and again. And all the while he never stopped touching her. He caressed the curve of her hips, cupped her buttocks in his palms, moved around to trace the line of her pelvic bone and sensitive area between her thighs.

He made her feel white-hot, all woman, as if their coming together like this had been inevitable from the first. "This skirt has to come off," he murmured.

A shiver of yearning swept through her as he unzipped it. She rested her hands on his shoulders as he drew the garment down her legs and helped her step out of it. Next he divested her of her black suede heels and tights, and when she was clad only in a black satin thong, from the waist down, she stopped him and said, "My turn."

He grinned. Off came his black pullover sweater. The snowy white T-shirt beneath. Although she was familiar with the buff shape of him—she had seen the imprint of his powerful muscles many times beneath his weekend T-shirts—it was the first time Holly had ever seen him bare-chested. His skin was golden and satiny smooth, covered with curling tufts of brown hair that spread across his pec's, before angling downward to his navel. Her heart racing, she unclasped his belt. His mouth moved on hers in a kiss that was shattering in its possessive sensuality. He caught her hand. "You're getting ahead of me."

She arced toward him, murmuring, "Travis…"

He chuckled softly, pressing his lips against her throat in a series of wet, hot kisses. "Ladies first." Off came her cranberry cashmere sweater. His eyes darkened with pleasure as he gazed at her breasts spilling out of her black satin demi-bra. Bending her backward, he traced the exposed slopes and valleys of her breasts before pushing aside one strap and then the other. As he peeled the fabric away from her nipples, sending her into a frenzy of wanting, he smiled tenderly. "You are so beautiful…"

Holly felt beautiful, inside and out. She sensed that if they were on the brink of the most important moment of their lives. Maybe love wasn't involved here, but everything else that mattered was present—to the point she was beginning to feel as if this coming together was a step toward something unexpectedly wonderful.

His lips closed over the tip of her breast, tugged gently. Sensation warred with the thrill of possession. His ministrations felt incredibly good, incredibly right. Holly clung to him and surrendered all the more. Pressing his manhood against her, hot and hard, Travis murmured in pleasure, then moved to her other breast, giving it the same fervid attention. When she could stand it no more his lips caught hers again. He kissed her wantonly, altering the angle, increasing the depth and torridness of their kiss. Her excitement mounted, fueled by the rasp of their breathing and the feel of his hard chest rubbing against the softness of hers. It was all she could do to remain on her feet.

His lips brushed across her collarbone, across the slope of her breasts, eliciting tingles of excitement everywhere they touched. His arms were strong, insistent, cocooning her in sensual pleasure. Holly closed her eyes and arched against Travis, the gentle eroticism of his touch flowing over her in warm, wonderful waves. Her senses spun as he finished undressing them both and drew her down to lie between the sheets on his bed.

He stretched out on his back and pulled her on top of him, his manhood pressing against the soft skin of her inner thighs. Kissing her all the while, he molded her breasts with his palms, circling the aching crowns, teasing the nipples into tight buds of awareness.

The kiss ended and he shifted her beneath him. His lips forged a burning trail down the slope of her neck, across the curve of one breast, then the other. She cried out as he moved lower still. Engaging every sense, he made his way slowly down her body, fulfilling every fantasy she had ever had. Trembling from head to toe at the long, sensual strokes of his tongue and the soothing feel of his lips, she caught his head in her hands, tangling her fingers in his hair. Holly moaned, knowing she wanted Travis as she had never wanted anyone before.

He stroked her hips and thighs as if she were the most precious thing in the world to him. He found her with his lips, tantalizing and exploring. Her head fell back; her body shuddered with pleasure. Need spiraled—and then blossomed—deep inside her. And then she came apart in his hands as unbelievable pleasure ricocheted within her.

Travis held her through the aftershocks, cradling her tenderly.

Relishing the no-holds-barred way he made love, determined to take him to the brink and show him the same loving care, she shifted positions. And took the lead, tracing his hot, satiny skin, learning the mysteries of him, as thoroughly and deliberately as he had just learned hers. Excitement built inside her, as she savored the sensation of enjoying someone—without restraint. And then there was no holding back for either of them. He needed to be a part of her as much as she needed him deep inside her. Emotions soaring, heart full, Holly accepted the warm, wonderful weight of him over her. His hands moved beneath her hips, lifting and positioning her. Holly felt his manhood poised to enter her, pulsing against her, and the climax she'd felt earlier came roaring back. She moaned as Travis buried himself in her, making it an all-or-nothing proposition with each slow, deliberate stroke. The gentle tenderness they'd experienced quickly turned to fierce abandon and stunning need.

Soaring with passion, Holly gave herself over to the hot kisses and hotter mating, moving her hips to the commanding rhythm of his until a cry of exaltation rose in her throat. She trembled and clenched around him. He dived deep. And then all was lost in the wild reckless turn their two-year friendship had inexplicably taken.

Chapter Six

It had been a long time, Travis thought, as his body relaxed and his breathing slowly returned to normal, since he'd felt as fortunate as he did at that moment. And it was all because of Holly. She was the one woman who understood he couldn't afford to be vulnerable to love at this point in his life. Holly supported his desire to focus on being a single parent, and stay rooted firmly in the here and now. His only immediate investment in the future pertained to his daughters and his business.

In return, he empathized with Holly's current aversion to risk. She had been hurt badly once; she didn't want to put herself out there and chance it happening again. She knew—as he did—that one day in the very distant future it might be possible for each of them to fall in love and marry again. But for the time being, this was the life they had—and both were determined to make the most of it.

And that, Travis knew, made them the perfect match. At least for now…

He sensed she felt the same way, judging by the aura of well-being emanating from the lithe body stretched out alongside his. Travis lifted her hand to his mouth, kissed it gently, then reached over and turned on the beside light. "What are you thinking?"

Holly rolled onto her side, facing him, and propped her head on her upraised hand. Although she was still as naked as he, the sheet was pulled up over her breasts. To his relief, she seemed as at ease now as she had been during their lovemaking. A gentle smile lifted the corners of her lips. "I was reflecting on the fact that I never realized how much I missed having sex until the first time you and I kissed." Her voice dipped a sultry notch. "And then, just like riding a bike…it all came back to me. So I began to think that maybe I could have it all—without going through the ordeal of dating or marrying again."

Was that what the act of courtship had been to her? Travis wondered. A hassle to be avoided like the plague? Had she been hurt, not just by Cliff's abandonment but throughout their entire relationship?

Holly was a low-key, low-maintenance woman who gave much more than she received. So if she felt that let down, Travis realized, Cliff must have really blown it with her, all along.

Oblivious to the depth of his concern, she ran a finger over Travis's rib cage, tracing idle patterns on his skin. "The thing is," she admitted, "I like the way I felt in your arms." She looked deep into his eyes and smiled. "Like a woman again."

He had liked the way she felt in his arms, too.

More than he had even imagined he would. And his imagination this last week had been a potent thing to overcome. "And I like being the man that made it all happen for you," he admitted with equal frankness, gathering her close once again.

She shifted, the silk of her hair brushing his chest. Taking nothing for granted, she asked, "To the point you'd be willing to do it again?"

Travis knew they had embarked on something special that far surpassed their wildest expectations. So despite the obvious risk this posed to their friendship, there was no denying this foray into passion was working out well thus far. He saw no reason it shouldn't be continued. "Anytime, anywhere," he teased.

Holly searched his eyes. "I'm serious." Her tone sobered. "Now that we've done the deed and had a moment to reflect, I'm asking you if tonight's activity was just a rebound thing, designed to help you get back in the saddle again and move on. Or if you would be content with something less grandiose than what you had when you were married to the love of your life?" Her casual, self-effacing tone hinted at the vulnerability she felt deep inside.

Travis sobered, too. "Or, in other words, am I willing to continue having sex with my very best friend?"

"I know it's not the same," she told him with the gentle compassion he loved so much.

Holly was right, Travis noted silently. What had happened tonight wasn't the same. He was beginning to realize, to his surprise, that in some ways it was better. His relationship with Diana had been all hearts and flowers, based more on the romantic accoutrements of marriage than the kind of in-the-trenches-of-single-parenting mode he and Holly had experienced together. The two of them had few illusions about each other, and that made their relationship strong. "You and I are like war buddies—soldiers bonded together in battle." With common experiences that would have been hard to explain to anyone else, never mind detailing their impact.

She grinned at the totally guylike analogy, then prodded, "Whereas you and Diana?"

"Each did our own thing," Travis recollected. Even after the girls had come along, their lives had remained largely separate much of the time. He had been focused on his work, true, but Diana had preferred to do most of the parenting her own way, with little or no assistance from him. Only after her death had Travis become such an involved dad. And he did regret that, looking back, thinking about how much he had missed in the first part of the girls' lives.

"Do you still miss Diana?"

There was no jealousy in Holly's voice, only gentle curiosity. Still, the question caught him off guard. Travis had to think before he could answer. "Actually, no," he said finally. "I did at first."

Holly released the breath she had been holding, wet her lips. "I remember."

"Now, it seems like my marriage was a lifetime ago."

Holly traced the fabric of the sheet with the same attention to detail she had shown making love. Her gaze dropped to the pensive movements of her fingertips. "Mine, too."

"Except your ex is about to make a return appearance in your life," Travis reminded her, surprised to feel a flare of jealousy.

Holly pursed her lips. "If my mother's instincts are right, Cliff won't stay around for long."

Travis hoped that was the case and not wishful thinking on her part. "The point is," she persisted, "what's going to happen to us now that we've rung this bell?"

"Well…" Travis smiled, amazed at how much joy this woman brought to his life. He rolled so she was beneath him once again. Keeping the bulk of his weight braced on his arms, he draped his body over hers, kissed his way from her ear to her cheek. "Since you can't unring a bell—" he paused to gaze into her eyes "—I say we stay the course and be together whenever we can. It'll be good for our health."

Holly chuckled. She pushed a playful palm against his chest and shifted positions, so she was astride him. She framed his face with her hands, kissed her way down his neck. "I've heard having sex can add years to your life," she teased.

Travis ran his palms down her spine, loving the shape of her body and the satin of her skin. "We're about to find out."

She caught her breath as he kissed her once more, then captured her breasts with his hands. "You're really going to make love to me again?"

"Yes," Travis said, "I am."

HOLLY ONLY MEANT TO cuddle with Travis for a few minutes after their second bout of truly magnificent lovemaking, before going next door to her own home and her own bed. But she must have fallen asleep, because the next thing she knew it was four in the morning and his phone was ringing.

Travis reached for it. "Hello?" He listened. "Sure. We'll be right there. Don't worry about it. I'll get her."

"The kids?" Holly guessed as soon as he hung up.

"They woke up. Sophie's happy, but Tristan, Tucker and Mia have decided they don't like sleeping over at someone else's house if we aren't there."

Holly grabbed her clothes and began to dress while Travis filled her in. "Apparently, Alexis called you first and couldn't get an answer over at your place."

Uh-oh. Holly flushed in embarrassment. "Do you think she suspects…that we…"

Travis shrugged, unconcerned. "Why would she? Up to now, the two of us have been just friends."

But Alexis was a veteran matchmaker and had told her point-blank that she sensed something more was on the way, Holly thought worriedly. She put on her sweater, then realized it was inside out and had to take it off again. She righted the garment, then struggled into it again. "I don't want people knowing."

Travis stepped behind her to help her with the zipper on her skirt. "That we're bed buddies? Don't worry. They won't hear it from me."

Unfortunately, it wasn't that simple, Holly soon discovered. No sooner had she and Travis walked in the door than Grady lifted a brow and sent a questioning look Travis's way. Was it that obvious, what they had been doing? She supposed so, given how relaxed and glowing they both appeared. Never mind that they had on the exact same clothes they'd worn to the party. That probably wouldn't have happened if she'd been at home sleeping in her own bed when the call came.

Mia ran to Travis, demanding to be picked up. "I had a bad dream, Daddy."

"I'm sorry to hear that, sweetheart. What was it about?" he asked compassionately.

"Santa Claus. He said he couldn't bring me a mommy."

At least they were getting the gist of what was plausible and what wasn't, Holly thought, slightly encouraged.

"But I told him I really *really* wanted one and he still said no! And that was when I started crying and waked up," Mia continued, with a sharp exhalation.

Sophie joined them. She tugged on Travis's pant leg. "So I told Mia that maybe Santa could bring us a mommy, after all."

"Honey," he said, looking pained. He hunkered down to meet both of them on their level, and went on in a low, understanding voice, as firm as it was gentle. "We've gone over this. It's not going to happen."

Tears of outrage rolled down Mia's cheeks. She began to wail.

"How about I go ahead and put her and Sophie in the SUV?" Travis raised his voice to be heard above the din.

Now that she was actually here, Holly noted, nonplussed, her sons seemed more interested in playing with Savannah McCabe's building block set than actually departing. "I'll get their coats on and meet you at the car," Holly promised. At that, Tucker and Tristan, began to cry.

Savannah and Kayla cried because everyone else was crying.

And that was the end to Holly and Travis's evening.

HOLLY'S PHONE RANG SHORTLY after one the following afternoon.

"How are things over there?" Travis asked.

"I'm great," Holly said. Still filled with that postcoital glow, she had breezed through her slated chores and activities, all the while thinking about when and where she and Travis might have a chance to hook up again. "Unfortunately, I can't say the same for Tucker and Tristan." She cringed as a fight threatened to break out over a favorite toy, and she headed that way.

The twins saw her coming with That Look, and the ruckus promptly quieted, thus avoiding the fifth time-out of the day so far.

Holly edged away, still keeping an eye on the boys, and continued in a voice only Travis could hear, "The twins never went back to sleep."

"Nor did Sophie and Mia," he murmured in commiseration.

Relaxing at the knowledge that he was always there for her, on those rough parenting days, Holly continued, "I was going to take Tucker and Tristan shopping, but something tells me it's not the right time to have them in a store—any store—selecting gifts. Never mind waiting in line at the cash register."

Travis chuckled. The masculine rumble warmed her insides. "They're a little cranky, I take it?"

"A lot, actually," she admitted. "Yours, too?"

"Ohhh yes. I think we're up to half a dozen time-outs so far, with more to come unless we change the mood around here."

"Gotcha."

"Think yours might be up for a little drive to look at Christmas decorations?"

Holly did a double take. "In broad daylight?"

"Desperate times call for desperate measures. And while the lights won't be on, they'll be able to see other things, like Santa's sleigh, and mangers."

It wasn't the first time the two of them had loaded all their kids in his nine-passenger SUV, but now that they had slept together, the event took on new meaning. It seemed more intimate somehow. Although it shouldn't, Holly told herself firmly. They had agreed last night that the sex between them was merely an extension of their close friendship, nothing more.

If Travis married again, as she suspected he eventually would, she knew that he'd want everlasting romantic love to be the basis of the union. And, Holly was beginning to realize, if it ever happened for her, she wanted real romance and enduring love this time, too. So as good as it currently was between her and Travis, it was based purely on friendship and physical passion. Long-term, she wanted what she had never had—the real deal.

"So what do you say?" Travis pressed.

Holly smiled and hazarded another look at her sleep-deprived children. "I know where you're going with this."

"It's one way to get them to nap," he admitted.

Half an hour and three long, winding tours around their North Richland Hills neighborhood later, all four of the children were sound asleep. Travis turned into his driveway and cut the motor. "Now for the real trick," he whispered, as Holly went ahead to open the door to her house.

Slowly, Travis eased Tucker out of his booster seat and carried him into the house, up the stairs, while she waited at the car in case anyone woke up. Travis returned and managed to lift Tristan out, too. Then Mia and Sophia. At last, all four preschoolers were napping soundly in their beds. Travis met Holly in the patch of grass between their driveways. "Mission accomplished," he said with a smile.

Holly nodded. A little disappointed that she hadn't thought to ask him to put his girls down for a nap at her house, so Travis and she could hang out together, she asked, "Want to get together later?"

"Actually…" He paused as Mrs. Ruley's car turned into the driveway and parked next to his.

Disappointment filtered through Holly at the sight of their shared weekday nanny getting out of her car. "You've got plans?"

He nodded. "For this afternoon."

To her frustration, he offered nothing more.

Holly had noticed Travis was more dressed up than usual. Instead of his weekend attire of jeans and a polo shirt, he was wearing brown dress slacks, a checkered button down shirt and loafers. She had attributed his care with grooming to what had happened between them the night before. She was in nicer than usual clothing, too. Obviously, though, his attire wasn't due to anything related to her. The fact that she had thought it was embarrassed her. Who was it that said sex changes everything? In their case, clearly it hadn't!

Still, this complication—if that was even what it was—shouldn't prevent her from seeking out Travis's company. "About dinner…?" she suggested cheerfully.

Again, Travis's guard was up. "I was going to ask Mrs. Ruley to do that for me and put the girls down early. But if you want the boys to come over and join them at my place…to give you a little extra time to yourself…"

"No. Honestly. That's fine. I need to get the twins down early tonight, too, since tomorrow is a school day.

And after they are asleep I'll be getting the paints together for the McCabe nursery mural, which I'm starting tomorrow."

Travis paused, looking conflicted, but giving her no further information about his undisclosed plans. "If you change your mind…"

Feeling foolish for having assumed too much, as well as a little hurt, she found herself backing away. Wasn't this what had happened with Cliff? Things had seemed fine, better than fine, then one day…they weren't. One day without warning she had turned into a complication in his life Cliff didn't want or need.

Holly swallowed. "I'll let you know." But even as she spoke, she knew she would not change her mind, or impose on Travis any more that day.

TRAVIS FELT BAD ABOUT the way things had ended with Holly. He could see he had flummoxed and disappointed her, and part of it was his fault. He should have come up with a plausible excuse for his absence. Not that he had to check in with her about where he was going or who he was seeing. They didn't need to ask each other's *permission* to do anything.

And honestly, if he and Holly hadn't made love for the first time last night, she probably wouldn't have given Mrs. Ruley's presence at his place a second thought. They were both free to pay the nanny overtime whenever they found the need, provided their sitter had time in her schedule.

But normally, especially at Christmastime, when there was so much extra to be done, he would have asked Holly in advance if she wanted to share in their nanny's services.

The reason he hadn't was because he didn't want to tell her where he was *really* going. After all, he had no idea how she'd react about him going downtown to talk to the P.I. he had hired to do the extensive background check on Cliff Baxter. So he planned to keep mum about all this unless the situation warranted her direct involvement.

Fortunately, Laura Tillman was right on time and waiting for him at her office. As Travis expected, the statuesque redhead got right down to business. "As I told you earlier in the week, the initial check on Cliff Baxter turned up nothing. He's as financially solvent as ever, still working for the same investment banking firm he was when he and Holly were married, although now he's a vice president. He's an only child, with the rest of his family deceased." She looked down at her dossier. "He's been in London, but is in the process of moving back to Connecticut, and has been spending some time reconnecting with a few of the friends he left behind— like his old college roommate, Simon Armstrong, an insurance exec who lives in Dallas."

Nothing there, Travis thought in frustration. He drummed his fingers on the arm of his chair. "What about his love life? Were you able to find out anything there?" Or in other words, did he want Holly back?

Laura drew a couple of black-and-white photographs out of a file folder. "My associate in the Connecticut area took these."

It was the first picture Travis had ever seen of Holly's ex. By the time he'd gotten to know her, the divorce was final, and she'd put all reminders of the man away. She'd never gotten any out to show her kids, because at three and a half, they had accepted the fact they didn't have a daddy—only a mommy—and she hadn't been forced to go down that road. Although one day soon they were going to have to engage in that discussion.

Travis didn't envy Holly that. He had no clue what she was going to say or how she was going to explain to the twins that their father wanted to see them after a prolonged absence.

"He's a good-looking guy, isn't he?" Laura remembered.

Travis glanced up. He had an idea where she was going with this. She knew him well enough to realize he was suffering pangs of unaccustomed jealousy over this situation.

But the truth was, Cliff *was* a good-looking man, in that elegant old money, boarding school kind of way. He had blond hair, like the twins, and the lean physique and year-round tan that came from spending summers yachting, and winters on the tennis courts and golf course.

Next to him was a self-assured, late-thirty-something woman with dark hair and eyes. She was model thin, wearing an elegant business suit, and what looked to be real jewels.

"That's Penelope Kensington."

The name meant nothing to Travis.

"She's the founder and CEO of the London Doll Company. Started fifteen years ago and now famous worldwide?"

Travis shrugged. His daughters liked dolls—the kind you could pick up at discount department stores.

"Apparently, Penelope and Cliff have been quite the item for about six months now. She's considering moving to the States to be with him."

Travis frowned. "Then why is he searching out Holly and the boys?"

"Not sure. Rumor is he wants to marry her, but she wants kids and isn't sure she is going to be able to have them."

Travis felt a sinking in his gut. "Tell me Cliff isn't going to try and get his sons back in order to give them to another woman!"

Laura Tillman shrugged, like the veteran P.I. she was. "It's almost too cruel to contemplate, isn't it?"

But stranger things had happened, they both knew.

HOLLY HEARD A CAR DOOR close at four o'clock. She looked out the window and saw Travis head inside his house. A couple of minutes later, he was at her front door. The expression on his face curiously introspective, he shoved his hands in the pockets of his pants. "How's it going?"

Still stinging over his perplexing behavior earlier, but trying to take it in stride, she attempted a casual attitude she couldn't begin to feel. "Things are okay," she reported matter-of-factly. "The twins woke up about half an hour ago and aren't too cranky yet."

"Same with my girls," Travis said, still looking as if he had much more on his mind than he wanted to say at that moment. "Mrs. Ruley made some ginger-bread men and wants to know if the twins want to come over to help decorate 'em while you and I run a special errand."

Special errand. That sounded mysterious. The sexy, expectant glimmer in his eyes upped her pulse another notch.

"And what would that be?" Holly murmured, as

Tucker and Tristan appeared on either side of her, hanging off of her.

"I'll tell you later," Travis said cryptically. He looked at her sons, asked cheerfully, "Want to come to our house and help decorate cookies?"

"Sure!" Tristan and Tucker exclaimed.

Travis knelt down far enough to scoop a twin in each strong arm, then headed off across the lawn. He called over his shoulder, "I'll be right back!"

Not sure what to make of his unusually high-handed manner, Holly brushed her hair and found her shoes. By the time she had located her house keys, he was back. "Ready to go?"

The day was unusually warm for mid-December— almost seventy degrees. The Texas-blue skies were cloud-free, the breeze just strong enough to feel good.

"Where are we going?" Holly stepped out beside him, happy to be with him once again.

And where were you earlier? And why do I have the sense that something is going on you don't necessarily want me to worry about?

"To see the playhouse and spaceship in progress. They're fully built—at least I think they are—but we haven't decided on paint colors, and I thought you might want to be involved with that."

"Absolutely." Excitement welled within her, and along with that, a huge burst of Christmas spirit.

Ten minutes later, they were in a large concrete building marked Carson Construction. Toward one end of the football-field-size warehouse was a clearing between sophisticated woodworking equipment and the custom cabinetry currently being constructed. He led her toward the stacks of premium wood and shelves of paint, wood stain and varnish.

The playhouse and spaceship were beautifully built, a child's dream. "What do you think?" Travis asked. "Did we get it right?"

Holly turned to him, thrilled beyond measure. "The kids are going to be ecstatic. So much so I don't know how we'll ever top it."

"I imagine we'll think of something next year," Travis said with a satisfied smile. He retrieved the file folder left next to the works in progress, and handed it to her. Enclosed were photos of the spaceship and playhouse, inside and out, and a palette of colors to choose from. "If you don't like any of those—all of which we have in stock—we can special order."

"No. This will be fine."

"Can you get me the specs by Tuesday? I know it's a rush job, but the sooner we get this completed, the better I'll feel."

"Me, too. No problem." Holly shut the file and looked up at him.

Because it was Sunday evening, they were the only two people there. The setting abruptly seemed intimate. To the point all she could think about was kissing him again.

Unfortunately, judging by the hesitant look in his eyes and the frown on his face, he wasn't thinking the same thing.

Instead, he took her by the hand and led her over to the break area, with its chairs and tables and vending machines. "Want a soft drink?"

Something seemed to be on his mind. Holly wondered if it had anything to do with his unexplained absence earlier that afternoon, his reason for getting Mrs. Ruley to babysit, without telling her. "A cherry Coke would be great."

He got two out of the machine and led her over to a table. He waited until they were settled opposite each other, then said, "I have something to tell you. And I'm not sure how you're going to feel about it."

Chapter Seven

THIS SOUNDS OMINOUS, HOLLY thought. Which was not a feeling she usually associated with her dealings with Travis. "Okay." She tried not to jump to conclusions. "I'm listening."

His dark brown eyes met hers. "This afternoon, I had a meeting with Laura Tillman, the private detective who does all the background checks on potential employees for me."

Holly shrugged. "Okay." She still didn't see what this had to do with her. Or why Travis looked so concerned.

His expression remained impassive. "I hired her to find out what she could about your ex-husband."

For a second, Holly thought she hadn't heard right. She leaned closer, struggling to understand.

"I wanted to know what's behind his sudden interest in seeing your kids," Travis explained brusquely.

Holly stared at him in disbelief. His actions went counter to everything she thought she knew about him. "Without consulting me?" She couldn't contain her hurt.

Travis nodded halfheartedly. "I wasn't sure you'd agree to it," he said finally. He leaned toward her and flattened both hands on the tabletop in front of him. "Hell, why not be honest? I wasn't sure *I* fully supported the decision."

That sounded like the man she knew. She hitched in a tremulous breath, aware this unfolding situation with her ex was going to force her to be stronger than she ever had been. "Then why did you go through with it?" she asked Travis.

His lips twitched. "Because I had to know," he said flatly.

Now, unfortunately, so did Holly. "And?" she asked, her heart pounding.

Briefly, Travis went over the facts the investigator had uncovered.

"So you think Cliff might want to start seeing the kids in order to give Penelope Kensington the family she has always wished for?" Holly guessed.

Travis tilted his head. "It would be one way for them to get what they want."

Holly shut her eyes, trying to reconcile the Cliff who had left her and the kids without a backward glance with the wannabe daddy Travis was describing.

She opened her eyes. "No…that's not it."

He lifted a brow. "How can you be so sure?"

"Because I know him." Holly flashed back on Cliff's refusal to even hold the twins in his arms more than once or twice. His feigned happiness when they were born, to his outright irritation when they woke him repeatedly with their crying at night. "I don't know what he's trying to achieve here," Holly said finally. "But I know in my gut he is no more interested in being a father now than he ever was."

"Then why does he want to see the twins?" Travis persisted.

Holding on to her composure with effort, Holly searched her mind for possibilities. Silence ticked out between them. "Maybe Cliff's concerned about the way the custody arrangement looks to others," she theorized eventually. "Or perhaps he's trying to impress a boss who has kids, in order to move up another rung on the career ladder." She paused for affect. "But whatever this is about, it's not about Cliff genuinely wanting to step up and be a father to the boys."

"You seem certain." It was Travis's turn to be surprised.

Holly sighed. Gulping back the anxiety rising up within her, she twined her fingers with his. "I've had a little over a week to think about it. And the message through Cliff's attorney, saying he wanted to bring presents, has kept me considering his motivations off and on all weekend." She'd put it out of her mind, only to start thinking about it again at some random time.

"And?" Travis looked down at their clasped hands.

Holly drew a deep, enervating breath. "I think, as much as it pains me to admit it, we're going to have to wait and see—and try not to let any of this ruin our holiday in the meantime."

Travis let his gaze drift slowly over her before returning to her face, then leaned across the table toward her. "Has anyone ever told you that you are a remarkably resilient woman?" he murmured.

Loving the way her hands felt in the comforting grasp of his, she smiled. "You have—at least a hundred times."

He grinned, pushed his chair away from the table, then shifted her out of her seat and onto his lap. Her arm immediately encircled his shoulders and neck as they got comfortable. Travis wrapped one arm about her back, the other around her waist. As their eyes met once again, he said, "That's only because I admire you so much."

"And yet—" Holly absently traced the shoulder seam on his shirt, knowing they had to talk about this, too "—you didn't feel comfortable enough to inform me what you wanted to do regarding the private investigator before you acted."

Travis clamped his lips together and remained unrepentant. "I didn't want to upset you if there was no need, and there was a chance absolutely nothing would turn up."

Trying not to notice how masculine and capable he looked in a warehouse setting, Holly slid off his lap and meandered over to the row of vending machines. She stared indecisively at the array of granola bars, chips and cookies. "Did you tell anyone else what you were doing?"

Travis stood, too, and sauntered closer. "Grady, Dan, Jack and Nate."

No surprise there. The five guys were not only business partners, they supported each other through thick and thin. Holly propped her hands on her hips. "I thought you and I had the kind of relationship where we could tell each other anything, too."

The corners of his lips curved upward. "We do."

"Then," Holly asked bluntly, "what's changed?"

MY FEELINGS, TRAVIS THOUGHT, leaning against the vending machine. *Without even thinking about it, I've started protecting you the way a man protects the woman he loves.*

But unable to tell Holly that without violating a very

fundamental tenet of their relationship, which was to keep things close but casual, Travis focused on what he could say to her.

"You and the boys have become such a big part of mine and the girls' lives. I don't want anything jeopardizing that," he said gruffly. *Especially not the louse of an ex-husband who didn't have sense enough to appreciate you and his kids in the first place.* "I love you all, Holly," Travis repeated emphatically.

Not, Holly noted sadly, "I love the boys and I'm *in love* with you." But "I love all of you."

What had she expected? she wondered miserably. For Travis to suddenly burst into some song and dance about how he was falling for her, as quickly and unexpectedly as she was falling for him?

Not very likely.

Aware that her own emotions were fast spiraling out of control, Holly swallowed. Said the words she was pretty sure Travis needed to hear, instead of the truer ones brewing deep inside of her.

"I love you and the girls, too, as friends and family." She looked him straight in the eye. *And I might be very, very close to falling in love with you.*

For both their sakes', however, she didn't tell him that.

Best to leave things as they were.

Travis went back to retrieve his soft drink. So did she. The silence between them felt awkward. His cell phone sounded an alert. He looked at the screen, picked up and read the text message.

Wordlessly, he showed the screen on his phone to Holly.

The SOS was from was Mrs. Ruley. At home, apparently all hell had broken loose during the cookie-decorating session, and she was calling for reinforce-ments, pronto.

"Guess we better go," Travis said.

"ASAP," Holly agreed.

TRAVIS WAS NOT HALF AS relieved by the timely interrup-tion as he should have been, because he felt things were left unsettled between the two of them.

The fact of the matter was he'd been out of line, hiring a private investigator to do some behind-the-scenes sleuthing regarding her ex-husband. Holly had had every right to be furious with him for messing in her business that way, yet she'd been more curious than annoyed. She had calmly given him a chance to explain—which he had—and then accepted thoughtfully what he'd revealed.

The right words had been said and peace had been restored…so why did he still feel so dissatisfied with the way their heart-to-heart talk had ended?

As they drove home in companionable silence, Holly seemed okay outwardly, Travis noted. It was inwardly, he deduced finally, that concerned him. It was clear from the pleasant but deliberately inscrutable expression on her face that she now had her guard up where he was concerned.

Travis supposed, on one level, he couldn't blame her.

He had taken her by surprise, going behind her back that way. He had stunned himself with his intimate involve-ment in what would normally have been someone else's problem, demanding no more than a sympathetic ear or a word of advice from him, had it been any other friend.

The thing was, Holly wasn't just any other friend, he realized with growing clarity.

She was more to him than that.

Much, much more.

"HE STARTED IT!" SOPHIE declared the moment Travis and Holly walked in the front door of his home.

"No, I didn't. She started it." Tucker was just as adamant.

"Actually," Mrs. Ruley intervened, from her place at the bottom of the stairs where the time-out for all four children was taking place, "it was pretty much an all-inclusive free-for-all. Needless to say," the nanny continued, eyeing the sulking, resentful expressions of all four children, "I couldn't take my eyes off them for one second until you got here to take over."

"No problem," Travis said. Exasperated by their behavior, which they clearly knew was wrong, he gazed at them sternly. "What do you have to say to Mrs. Ruley?"

Silence.

Travis arched a brow, as did Holly. "We're waiting," she said, backing him up the way he always backed her up in these challenging situations.

Big sighs resulted. "We're sorry," Tucker growled, sounding anything but.

"Try that again," Holly ordered firmly with another reprimanding lift of her brow.

"I'm sorry," Tucker said sincerely.

"Tristan?" she prompted.

"I'm sorry, too." He sounded contrite, but continued to scowl.

"Sophie?" Travis commanded.

The four-and-a-half-year-old's lower lip shot out. "Fine," she pouted cantankerously. "I'm sorry, too!"

"That didn't sound like a sincere apology," he observed.

Sophie lowered her eyes and said meekly, "I'm sorry." She sounded truly apologetic this time.

"Me, too. I'm sorry," Mia said.

A collective sigh of relief followed. None of the children liked getting into trouble, and they usually took pains to avoid it.

Mrs. Ruley turned to Travis and Holly. "If you've got this handled…"

The two of them exchanged glances and agreed. "We'll see you tomorrow morning," Travis said.

With a commiserating sigh, the nanny grabbed her coat and purse and headed out to her car.

The kids remained on their individual steps on the staircase. "Anyone want to tell me what this was about?" Travis asked, lounging against the wall.

Holly waited on the other side of the stairs, her back to the curving end of the oak banister. It was times like this that she really appreciated not having to parent entirely on her own, but could rely on Travis for backup.

Tucker spoke first. "We said we needed to ask Santa to help us find a daddy for Christmas, too, and Sophie said we don't because we already have one! But we don't have a daddy, do we, Mommy?"

Oh, dear, Holly thought. She really should have handled this a lot earlier.

When they'd been infants, she'd had no words that would have adequately explained what Cliff had done, in abandoning them, so she had simply told her children they lived in a house with a mommy and two little boys. Since the family next door was comprised only of a daddy and two little girls, it had seemed a "normal" situation to them. Now that they were three and a half, and midway through their first year of preschool, they were beginning to notice that some families had two parents. But they hadn't questioned why *they* didn't. Until now.

"Actually—" Holly took a deep breath "—you do have a daddy." She had known for a week now she had to talk to them about the fact that Cliff wanted to visit, but she hadn't because she kept hoping her ex-husband would chicken out again before next weekend rolled around.

"No, we don't!" Tristan argued logically. "We never seen one!"

"You *have* never seen one," Holly corrected automatically. "And that's because your daddy has been working very very far away."

"So is he coming for Christmas?" Tucker asked curiously.

Like it or not, maybe now was the time to broach the subject she had been dreading. "Yes," Holly said, curtailing her own reluctance—for their sake—and replacing it with a cheerful tone. "He is."

"When?" Tristan demanded.

"Next weekend, if all goes according to plan," she replied.

"Is he going to bring presents?"

Holly crossed her fingers that intent translated into action where Cliff was concerned. "He said he might." If not, she'd have something stowed away just in case.

"Oh."

Tristan turned to Sophie. "How come you know'd we had a daddy and we didn't?"

"I told her that a long time ago," Travis interjected, sending a look of apology Holly's way. "The beginning of the school year, I think. When Sophie's class was doing a unit on family, she asked if the twins' dad was deceased, like her mom, and I explained. And we went on to talk about other things." He winced, obviously feeling contrite. "The subject never came up again and I never gave it a second thought."

"So we're going to have a mommy and a daddy now," Tristan deduced.

"Because Kayla says having a mommy and a daddy at the same time is the bestest thing," Sophie interjected in excitement. "And Savannah says so, too. She really likes having Alexis as her mommy."

"We want a mommy and a daddy, too," Mia declared.

Sophie spoke for the entire group. "And that's all we want for Christmas!"

"Talk about a one-track mind!" Travis murmured in an aside to Holly.

They shared a look of mutual consternation, then he said, "This calls for a family meeting in the living room." He herded all the children to sit on the sofa, then took a seat on the thick leather-bound steamer trunk that served as a coffee table in the more formal, but still masculine surroundings.

Holly sat next to him on the trunk, facing the kids.

Travis braced his forearms on his spread knees and leaned forward. "I thought we were past this," he said.

Sophie and Mia exchanged looks indicating that was definitely not the case. Tucker and Tristan took their lead from the girls.

It was clear the kids had their minds made up. They wanted what they wanted. So Travis talked. Holly persuaded. Together, they both cajoled. All to no avail. The four children remained convinced that the best thing in the world would be to have a mommy and a daddy at the same time instead of one or the other.

And really, Holly thought, who could blame them?

Wasn't that what every child wanted? What most of their friends at preschool had? A complete family? In the boys' case, by having their dad stay on and live with them, and in Travis's…since Santa could not bring a mommy, by him finding a wife to marry….

Finally, in exasperation, Travis said, "Look, I understand the girls feel like they are missing out by not having a mommy, and the boys feel like they are missing out by not having a daddy, so how about we all stop trying to focus on what we don't have and instead come up with a different plan that will meet everyone's needs?"

Four sets of brows furrowed as the children regarded him warily. Clearly, the question was far too complex for them to grasp, but Holly got it, and the excess wordage did have the consequence of stopping their interruptions midsentence as they tried to comprehend what he meant.

"What did you have in mind?" Holly asked Travis, trusting it was good.

He turned toward her, his muscular thigh nudging hers. "Simply that whenever the boys have something that requires a daddy, I step in to help them out. And whenever the girls have a situation that demands a mommy, you step in."

Holly picked up the baton and ran with it. "It'll be sort of like having a next-door mommy and a next-door daddy," she said.

The children briefly looked intrigued.

The interest faded as quickly as it appeared.

"No," Sophie said, stubborn as ever. "I want my own mommy."

"Me, too," Mia agreed.

"And we want our own daddy," Tristan said.

And that, it seemed, was that.

"WE TRIED TO EXPLAIN," Travis said wearily, thirty minutes later. He had sent the children out to the backyard for fifteen minutes of playtime before dinner, so they could have a chance to figure out what they were going to do next.

Holly helped herself to one of the gingerbread men the kids had decorated with Mrs. Ruley. "And did not succeed."

Travis munched on a cookie, too. "Once they see their real gift from us—the playhouse and the spaceship— they'll forget all about this mommy and daddy business. And I meant what I said in there." He inclined his head in the direction of the living room. "I am available to your boys whenever they need an on-premises daddy."

"And I am, of course, available to your girls," Holly said.

"See?" Travis polished off the last of the cookie. He reached into the fridge and brought out a bag of premade salad mix and a jar of applesauce. "Problem already solved."

Holly's maternal intuition told her it was not going to be that simple. She took the opposite tack, in an effort to be prepared for any eventuality. "And if it's not?" She reached for the bottle of olive oil and vinegar on the counter, added salt and pepper to the group. "If despite all the ways and times we've tried to reason with them, and they're still expecting to have a complete family on Christmas Day? What then?" *Do we just let them be terribly disappointed?*

Travis handed her a mixing bowl and whisk. "Then we move on to plan B."

Trying not to think about the way he looked at her—as if she were suddenly the most fascinating woman on the planet—Holly began putting together a simple dressing for the salad. "And what might that be?" she bantered back.

Pleasure teased the corners of his lips. "We make arrangements to give them what they want most—at least for Christmas morning."

She really shouldn't be enjoying these interactions with him quite so much. Never mind anticipating more! She watched as he poured salad mix into a wooden bowl. "And how do we do that?" she asked, forcing herself to sound casual.

He set the bowl down next to where she was working and leveled a glance her way. "By joining forces and spending Christmas together."

The image of all of them gathered around the Christmas tree was unbearably exciting. Especially since, prior to this, they'd spent the holidays separately. Holly whisked in the seasoning, then poured dressing over the salad. She slanted him a sideways glance. "So we'd be one big happy family?" Just like the kids wanted…and her, too, if she was honest.

Travis shrugged and folded his arms in front of his chest. "I can't think of a better way to make the children's wishes come true, at least for the holiday. Can you?"

TRAVIS HAD THOUGHT—OR maybe just hoped—that Holly would jump at the idea of spending Christmas Day together. Instead, she looked as if he had just offered to give her a tetanus shot she didn't really need. Finally, she forced a smile. "It sounds like a good idea."

"It is," he said confidently. "So why are you hesitating?"

She raked her teeth across her lower lip. "You and I are starting to depend on each other an awful lot, Travis."

She made it sound like a negative. And maybe, given her need to maintain her independence and never again let her happiness depend on anyone but herself, it was.

But he wasn't just any guy.

He wasn't unreliable.

Travis clamped his hands on her shoulders. The move forced her to look him in the eye. "That's more or less the way it's always been for us, hasn't it? I borrow a cup of sugar from you. You call me when the kitchen sink needs unclogging."

She stepped back, as if suddenly afraid to be close to him. "This is different," she said quietly.

He could tell he'd touched a nerve. "In what way?"

Her aquamarine eyes took on a troubled sheen. "In the way that is great as long as neither of us is in another relationship, but would be a definite detriment to either of us becoming successfully involved with anyone else."

Travis took the casserole dish out of the oven to cool. "I don't want to start dating again at this point." Maybe never. Especially if it meant giving up all he shared with Holly. "You know that." Marriage—for either of them—was a very long way down the road.

Holly dressed the salad with single-minded focus.

"You could change your mind. Especially now that you and I have started…um…"

He guessed where this was going. "Making love?"

She nodded, pink creeping into her cheeks.

As if now that their self-imposed sexual droughts had ended, the floodgates would open, and they'd become so randy they'd lose all common sense. He surveyed her bluntly, figuring it best to get it all out in the open. "Are you saying you want to date other people?"

"No." The flush in her cheeks deepening, she carried the salad bowl to the breakfast room table. "Heavens no!"

It had to be said. "Cliff then?"

She gave him a startled look, her eyes seeming to hold more secrets than before. "A hundred times no!"

Jealousy roiled in his gut. "Sure about that?" She had never really talked about her previous marriage except to say it was over. Travis understood and accepted that, because he had no desire to talk about his late wife. Now, with Cliff about to make another appearance, maybe it was time they delved a little deeper. She seemed to think so, too, because she said, "I don't want to be dependent again on anyone who might leave."

Travis watched her come toward him once more. "I'm not going anywhere."

Holly stopped just short of him. She slanted her head, as if looking at him from that angle would give her a better understanding of what was going on inside him. Silky hair fell across her shoulder, onto her breast. The corners of her lips quirked. "You know what I mean," she chided softly.

And she had to know what he meant, Travis thought, taking a step closer. "I'm not going anywhere," he repeated, even more quietly. And then to prove it, he took her into his arms and kissed her soundly. Kissed her until her resistance faded and she was pressed against him in sweet surrender, returning each passionate caress.

And it was then that Travis became aware of patting and tugging on his leg. He broke off the kiss, looked down. Tristan, Tucker, Sophie and Mia were surrounding them. Cherubic faces tilted upward. "Whatcha doing?" Tristan asked.

Her lips still damp from his kisses, Holly blushed bright red. "We were, um…"

"Just testing out the mistletoe," Travis improvised quickly.

The kids looked around. "Mistle—what?"

Holly rolled her eyes, a response only he could see. Determined to protect their privacy, and the blossoming feelings between them, Travis continued his explanation with poker-faced authority. "We haven't hung it yet. We're just trying to figure out where it should go, when we get some."

All four kids studied him, with varying degrees of suspicion. "What's mistletoe?" Sophie asked.

"It's a little green plant that grown-ups hang at Christmas time as an excuse for kissing people. Although," Travis continued, dropping down to the children's height, "little ones who stand under it get more than kisses," he reported solemnly.

Tiny brows knit in confusion.

"What do they get?" Mia asked at last.

"Tickled!" Travis shouted.

The kids screamed in delight, sensing what was

coming, and then spread outward, scrambling to begin the game of chase.

"It's the Tickle Monster!" they yelled as Travis dashed after them, and the Q and A session came to an abrupt end.

Holly laughed and shook her head. "Boy, did you luck out," she called after him.

Travis grinned. Didn't he know it.

Chapter Eight

Travis met the guys on Monday evening to transport all the items donated by their employees to the Salvation Army collection center, for distribution over the holidays. Travis supplied the big construction truck. Volunteer employees from their businesses showed up to help load and unload. By nine o'clock, they were finished, so the five of them went to their favorite sports bar to watch the rest of the Cowboys football game.

Between plays, Travis told them about the latest turn in his little girls' efforts to find themselves a mommy in time for Christmas, and his proposed solution to the dilemma.

Like Holly, his pals seemed to have deep reservations about his idea.

The four guys exchanged looks. A raised brow or two was added to the mix.

Wordlessly, Nate helped himself to the chicken wings in the center of the table. He drizzled on a little shower of blue cheese dressing, to cool the heat. "What was Holly's answer?" he asked finally.

That was just it, Travis thought in frustration. "She hasn't given me one."

"Did she say why?" Jack wondered.

This was the part that really stung. "She thinks we're starting to rely on each other too much."

"And you don't agree." Grady commandeered the plate of nachos, dripping with cheese, beans and jalapeños. He added sour cream, pico de gallo and guacamole to the serving he heaped on his plate.

Travis sipped his beer and forked up a bite of southwestern eggroll, stuffed with grilled chicken, black beans, cheese and chilis. "I think things are great between us." Especially, he amended silently, now that they had started making love. He hadn't realized how much he had missed the physical closeness until he held Holly in his arms. Now that he knew, wondering when they would have the chance to be together again was all he could think about….

"Why don't you just put yourself out of your misery and tell her how you feel?" Dan suggested.

"We can all see you've got a thing for her," Jack said.

How many times was he going to have to repeat this? Travis wondered. "We're friends."

Another round of "looks" passed around the table. A roar went up as the Cowboys scored, taking the lead. Travis and his friends added to the hooting and hollering, much to the dismay of the Saints fans in the bar. Then Grady cleared his throat. "Let me ask you this. How would you feel if Holly started dating someone else?"

That was easy, Travis thought. He'd feel terrible. Out loud, he had a much cooler response. "Depends on who it was," he said with an offhand shrug.

Skeptical glances abounded. "If she went back with her ex-husband, now that he's prowling around?" Grady pressed.

"Even worse," Travis said, able to be completely honest this time. "Given how Cliff treated her before."

Dan smiled. "How would she feel if you started dating someone else?"

Ah. The fifty-million-dollar question. "I don't know." He shrugged. "I suppose she would have to give her approval, in the way that close friends and family do, just as I'd have to give my approval to her, if she ever wanted to go down that road."

A groan went round the table that had nothing to do with the Cowboys interception and subsequent fumble on the fifty yard line. "I hate to tell you this, friend—" Dan slapped Travis on the shoulder "—but you are in love with that woman."

He scowled, disagreeing. "I love her like a…"

"Like a what?" Nate asked impatiently.

Travis tried to say "friend." For the first time, the word wouldn't come out. "I'm not denying we're close. Or that I love her the way you love anyone you spend a lot of time with. But as for being in love with her…" Guilt and confusion warred inside him. He struggled to explain. "What I feel for Holly doesn't begin to compare with what I felt for Diana."

The expressions on his friend's faces grew compassionate. They waited while, with difficulty, Travis expounded, "Romantic love involves a lot of highs and lows." He swallowed, thinking about some of the fights he'd had with Diana, the way he'd always had to be careful what he said or did, so as not to set her off, and be relegated to sleeping on the sofa again. "It's never been like that with Holly. With her, it's always been so easy."

"In what sense?" Nate, the bachelor asked.

Travis shrugged. "I can tell her anything."

"And with Diana?" Grady probed.

"She wanted a knight in shining armor. I tried to give her that."

"So you never told her about the worries you had during the lean years, when you were expanding the family business to what it is today," Jack figured.

With good reason, Travis thought, helping himself to another chicken wing. "Diana wouldn't have been able to sleep at night."

"And Holly?" Nate polished off the nachos.

Travis reflected. "She's obviously tough enough to take pretty much anything, as has been evidenced by the way she's handling her ex-husband's attempted reentry into her life."

"How's that situation going, by the way?" Grady asked.

Travis brought them all up to date, feeling proud of the way that had worked out. "So even there, I was able to tell Holly what I'd done, and she was cool with it. She didn't hold my meddling in her private affairs against me."

"Which again says something," Dan observed.

Travis lifted a questioning brow.

"She loves you," Dan stated.

"And how do you know that?" he demanded.

"Because," Nate said sagely, reaching for the last of the wings, "she never would have tolerated such interference from 'just a friend.'"

The guys couldn't be right about that, Travis thought, as he drove home an hour later.

Because it was a school night, and Mrs. Ruley had already worked an entire day, Holly had agreed to keep the kids for him. She'd put them to bed in the twins' room. The plan was he would collect them before breakfast the next morning and see them off to preschool.

He often did the same for her, if she was working late for a client, trying to finish a mural.

Tonight, instead of going home to his empty house, right to sleep, he wanted to talk with Holly. The fact that her studio lights were on had him picking up his cell phone to text her.

Still up? he wrote.

She texted back. Yes. Have something to show you. Now okay?

Now, Travis thought, was great.

HOLLY WENT DOWNSTAIRS TO open the door, sketch pad in hand. Thinking nothing of the tank top and loose, flowing knit pajamas she wore, or the cardigan thrown over top of them for warmth, she padded in her sock-clad feet down the stairs to let Travis in.

He looked as handsome as ever, with his cheeks ruddy from the cold night air, his hair windblown, his eyes intent and oh, so dark and sexy. The collar of his suede jacket was turned up against the strong column of his throat. Behind him, the night was lit by the twinkling multicolored Christmas lights throughout the neighborhood. If Holly hadn't known she was imagining it, she would have sworn she heard Christmas bells ringing.

"I'm so glad you came by!" she said, excited by the work she had done on behalf of their kids. "I know we

were talking about a simpler approach, but I was thinking it might be nice to paint on a fancy control panel in
the twins' backyard spaceship, and do a 'room background' mural in the interior of the playhouse."

She showed him the sketches.

The approval in his expression warmed her through
and through, and told her he thought she was onto something, too, turning up the volume a notch.

"All I'll need is about six hours, once the rest of the
basic painting is done, and I selected the colors for that,
too." She turned a page of her sketchbook and showed
him her choices.

"Nice," Travis said.

"So you think we have time to get this all done in the
next ten days?"

He nodded. "I can have the base colors on both applied
tomorrow. Just let me know what evening you want to do
the mural artistry. I'll line up Mrs. Ruley to sit for us, and
go with you. The regular cabinetmakers and warehouse
crew go home at six, so any time after that is fine."

Holly consulted the calendar she kept on her phone.
"Wednesday okay?"

"Works for me," he agreed.

"I was just about to have milk and cookies," she told
him, tempting him with a playful waggle of her brows.
"Want some?"

"Always." Travis shrugged out of his jacket and hung
it on the coat rack in her foyer, the way he had hundreds
of times before.

And yet, as Holly led the way back to her cozy
kitchen, the casual action felt different tonight, more
intimate. Maybe because they had made love. And were

contemplating doing it again, when the time and mood were right. But for tonight, cookies and milk would have to satisfy their craving. "So how was your evening with the guys?" she asked cheerfully.

"That's what I wanted to talk to you about," Travis said. He settled on a stool at the island, while she got out a silver cookie tin, jug of milk and two glasses.

She rounded the island, settled on the stool next to him and pried open the lid. The aroma of confectioner's sugar, butter and pecans wafted up to tickle their noses. "Mexican wedding cookies!" he stated.

"I know. And they're to die for." Preferring to concentrate on the treat, rather than the other possibilities lingering in the back of her mind, she lifted one to his lips.

He took a bite. "Delicious."

She grinned and touched the tip of her index finger to the corner of his mouth, wiping away a dab of powdered sugar. Then she sat back, secretly thrilled to have him there with her. "I'm listening," she said.

Shifting in his seat, Travis said, "They all think I'm love in with you."

TRAVIS'S WORDS AFFECTED HOLLY the way he expected they would. She paused, cookie halfway to her mouth. *"What?"*

"I know." He was relieved she felt the same way. He sat back, trying to ease the pressure at the front of his jeans. "It's ridiculous, isn't it?"

"Totally!" Holly agreed with a deliberate shake of her head, her golden-brown hair cascading over her shoulders. "What we have is so much more than that!"

More? Than romantic love? Suddenly confused,

Travis asked, "Isn't that supposed to be the epitome of what women want?"

Holly sipped her milk. "Not me," she said firmly. "I had romantic love with Cliff. The perfect courtship. Wonderful wedding. Happiness personified for the first five years of our marriage."

These were the kind of details he had been searching for. "And then what happened?" Travis asked, wanting to make sure that whatever mistakes Cliff had made would not be repeated by him.

Abruptly, some of the light left her eyes. She looked sad and tense. "He wanted to have a baby."

Travis studied her anguished expression. "Cliff?"

She shrugged, looking even more uncomfortable. "I know. Ironic, isn't it? But yes, he was the one who first brought it up. He thought with our careers flourishing, that it was time to have one child. Not two. One."

Travis turned his glance away from the soft, erratic rise and fall of her breasts. Ignoring his instinct—which was to pull her into his arms and hold her close until the hurt she had suffered went away—he continued, "So when he found out you were having twins…"

Holly made a face. "He wasn't happy. I mean, he *said* he was, but…I could see beneath the superficial veneer that he was having second thoughts."

Travis worked to contain his disgust. Had he been the father, he would have been shouting his joy to the world, right along with Holly. Instead, she had been made to feel guilty about it. Still, Travis tried to give the guy the benefit of the doubt. Maybe there had been more on Cliff's mind than either of them knew. "Did you ask him about it?" he asked casually.

Pain clouded her eyes. "Nope."

Travis studied the golden lights shimmering in her brown hair. "Why not?"

She slowly let out her breath, then rubbed the smooth surface of her white-painted breakfast table. "We didn't have that kind of marriage. We didn't look at the dark corners or the places where the seams were beginning to fray. We just focused on the illusion of perfection." She lifted her gaze and continued with self-effacing honesty. "And I'm as much at fault as he was in this, I'm an artist who deals in beautiful things and I wanted my fairy-tale life through and through."

Travis understood that. He and Diana had done pretty much the same thing, albeit for different reasons. "So how'd you get from there to the end of the road?" he asked Holly gently, glad they had the time and opportunity to finally talk about this.

Sadness crept into her low tone. "It was a gradual erosion over the course of my entire pregnancy. I kept seeing the doubts Cliff was trying to hide, and kept ignoring them. Focusing instead on trying to create the perfect twins' nursery…and waiting to learn the sex of the babies, in hopes that the surprise of the moment would make the birth all the more magical."

"But it didn't."

She shook her head, disappointment and regret evident in the tortured grimace on her face. "The truth is, nothing would have worked. And you know why?" Her expression became inherently stubborn once again. "Because Cliff and I based our relationship on romantic love. And that's nothing but an illusion. Illusions can't last, especially not when confronted with the wear and tear of everyday living and familiarity."

"Exactly why Diana insisted the two of us maintain separate bathrooms." She had wanted to preserve the "mystery." And although it had worked to a certain degree, it had also failed them, in upholding boundaries that usually were done away with during the course of a long and satisfying marriage. There was an intimacy that came from sharing the same space when you got ready to go to work, or to bed at the same time. He and Diana had never had that. Travis was beginning to see that, as good as his marriage had been, it had also been lacking in ways that would have hurt them over the long haul...

An awkward silence fell. Finally, Holly cracked a joke. "Maybe if I'd gone that route, I'd still be married."

From what she had just related, Travis doubted it. But it did raise an interesting question. "Do you still want to be married?" he asked.

That, at least, seemed easy enough for her to answer. "No," she said flatly. "Nor do I ever want to fall in love again or trust that anything will last forever. Not when I know in my heart it just won't. And I thank my lucky stars that you feel the same way I do," she added.

But did he really still feel that way? Travis wondered. Or was he simply agreeing with Holly to keep from alienating her?

Travis sighed. While he couldn't deny there was a certain safety in trying to keep things the same, wasn't a static relationship of any kind doomed to fail?

He massaged his temples. All this back and forth was giving him a headache.

All he knew for sure was that Holly and Cliff had not

grown and changed in the same ways at the same time, and their marriage had ultimately failed.

He didn't want to lose his closeness with Holly for that or any other reason.

Therefore, the two of them had to stay on the same page—and the page she was on said no romantic love and no marriage.

"You need to tell your guy friends they're on the wrong track regarding us," Holly advised when he finally met her eyes.

Travis decided that he would ignore all the advice he was getting from well-meaning friends, and focus instead on giving Holly what she felt she needed. "I will." he promised, reaching over to squeeze her hand.

Relief showed in her slender frame and a smile lit up her face. "Because you and I have all we need in our relationship to be happy right now. Food, friendship, and one of these days again, when mood and timing equal opportunity—" she wrinkled her nose at him playfully "—sex!"

Travis stood. Grasping her wrist, he drew her out of her seat and pulled her against him. Her arms wreathed his neck and she went up on tiptoe as he gave her a thorough, demanding kiss that spoke volumes about what he wanted and needed from her.

Unfortunately, although he felt her desire, he also felt the resistance. He drew back to read her expression. "I guess tonight…?"

She splayed her fingertips across his chest, and murmured with obvious regret, "As much as I'd really like to continue what we started the other night, I'm not sure I feel comfortable with the kids upstairs." Her lips twitched. "You know how they talk at preschool. And if even one of our kids were to wake up and find you here…"

Travis understood where she was going with this. "Who knows what they would say?" He had only to think about the request to Santa, in front of the news crew at their school, to realize what havoc loose talk could bring.

"We should wait until we have the time and place to do it right," Holly continued.

Travis savored the warmth of her slender body pressed against his. "I agree." He threaded a hand through her hair and gazed into her eyes. "So how about a noontime rendezvous?"

HOLLY COULDN'T BELIEVE SHE was actually doing this. Taking off work at lunchtime to meet Travis in a room at a posh downtown hotel. But here she was, at eleven forty-five on a Tuesday, freshly changed out of her mural-painting clothing into a pretty black pencil skirt, heels and Pacific-blue silk blouse. A blue-and-black necklace and earrings complemented the outfit. Her best black lace bustier and matching thong lay against her skin, reminding her with every step she took that she was about to become the kind of woman who put sex on her weekly schedule. Not with a husband, but with a friend and lover…and she was okay with that. More than okay, as it turned out.

Smiling, Holly strode into the hotel and went on up to room 324, where Travis was supposed to be waiting. She knocked once and then knocked again.

Nothing.

From behind her, a waiter approached, wheeling a room service cart. "Mrs. Carson?" he asked.

For a second, Holly had to think. So this was Travis's room, since the waiter had just mistaken her for his wife. She did her best to suppress a self-conscious blush. "Right. I don't have a key…and he's not answering."

"That's okay. The concierge is expecting him to be late arriving. I can get you in." The busboy used a passkey and wheeled the cart inside the elegant suite. "Your husband sent a message that you can start dining without him, if you wish. He'll be along shortly."

O-kay, Holly thought, wondering if Travis's late arrival was some sort of sign that all was not going to go smoothly today. She tipped the busboy. He thanked her and left.

Wondering what was going on, Holly checked her cell phone for messages. Nothing. No calls or texts. Perplexed, she took off her coat, began to pace.

She didn't normally wear bustiers or thongs these days, and they felt a little uncomfortable. Imagining Travis's surprise, she smiled. Moments later, she headed over to the window and checked the bedside phone. No messages there. Back to the room service cart. On it was an expensive bottle of champagne, perfect for celebrating. Under silver domes were an array of fresh fruit, several different types of cheeses and breads, and some decadent desserts.

Holly popped a delicious grape into her mouth, waited, and then ate some more.

Eventually, a half hour passed. And then an hour. Until there was no denying it—she had been stood up.

Chapter Nine

Holly had just resumed her place in front of the mural she was creating for Grady and Alexis McCabe's baby-to-be when she heard the front door of their elegant home open. "Good luck, buddy," she heard Grady say.

Another voice murmured something back before the door shut. The rumble of a car engine starting signaled that Grady was headed out for his business meeting. So Holly knew she and the interloper were alone when footsteps sounded on the stairs. A second later, Travis stood framed in the nursery doorway.

Although he was dressed professionally, she had never seen him looking more out of his element. He had a big black stain that resembled motor oil across the middle of his hopelessly wrinkled dress shirt, and his expensive shoes were caked with mud. He smelled of man and sweat. And still looked determined to have his way with her.

"No," Holly said. *A thousand times no.* There was no way she was giving him another chance to crush her hopes.

Travis lifted his hand in the age-old gesture of peace. "At least hear me out."

Holly shot him a drop-dead look. "Why should I after the way you humiliated me?"

He moved to stand where she couldn't help but see him, and lifted a brow as if the outcome of this brouhaha was already decided. "Because you know me well enough by now to realize that I have never stood you up before, and I sure as heck would not have picked today to start if the situation had been at all within my control."

The truth of his words slowly melted her resistance. She sighed, her anger and resentment turning to exasperation and regret. "What happened?"

He shook his head in mute condemnation and braced himself against the wall opposite the one she was painting. "The day started off fine. I made arrangements with the hotel. Rearranged my schedule to make sure I could get over there in plenty of time, and went to my first meeting of the day." He continued in a voice simmering with frustration. "Halfway through that, I get a call from Grady that the fund-raising committee for the new opera hall has decided they want to meet with all the groups vying for participation in the project. Our archrival, the Midtowne Development Group, already met with them and apparently wowed them while at the same time denigrating us—and they wanted to meet with us right away at the Cattleman's Club."

Holly had always known Travis was competitive, but prior to this, his drive to succeed had never gotten in the way of their friendship. And the stakes had never been this high for the two of them before. For the first time, she had an inkling of what a woman in his life might face, given the fact that if there was a competition, he had to emerge the winner. Deciding she needed to know more before she decided whether to let him off the hook, she said, "When you say 'us' you mean…?"

Travis stepped closer, his tall, strong body exuding so much heat he could have started a bonfire all on his own. "The usual group. Grady, Jack, Nate, Dan and me. Anyway," he continued, "they asked us to all swing by the Cattleman's Club for coffee at 10:00 a.m." He kept his eyes locked on hers. "I could have bowed out or sent someone in my stead, but I know those guys and their wives, and if an underling shows up, you're out of the running. They only want to meet with the top dogs."

"Go on," Holly urged impatiently, after he paused for an excruciatingly long moment.

He exhaled and continued in a flat, businesslike tone. "So I tell Grady okay, but I've got a lunch at twelve-thirty with you and I want to be out of there by eleven-thirty at the very latest. So if that means we wrangle them for a private dinner or something later, then that's what we'll do. Everyone agrees…." He cleared his throat. "We go over there and find out just how competitive it is going to be to win this thing. But okay, we're up for it. We give our collective pitch. They seem equally impressed with our group, especially the work we're doing at One Trinity Place, keeping the quality high and the budget in place."

"Sounds like you had a promising meeting," Holly said generously. "So, to make a long story short, did you just lose track of time?"

"Not exactly…" He winced. "So we start to leave and it's now eleven forty-five, and I'm in a hurry and trying not to act like it. Just as I'm about the make my big escape, I get waylaid by a couple of wives. They've all seen the local news story about the mommy that Mia and Sophie want Santa to bring us…and they think it's *so cute*."

Uh-oh, Holly thought.

"And their hearts all go out to me and the girls, and now they want me to participate in this silent auction they're having at the Kimball Museum Saturday night."

That didn't sound so bad so far, Holly thought, wary of any further attempts to find Travis a "wife" in time for the holiday.

Travis sighed warily. "All the proceeds are going for Christmas at the Baptist Children's Home, so I say sure."

Which made sense, Holly thought. Travis was a very generous guy.

"They want to give me details, but I say I don't have time—just call my office with them and I'll be happy to help. This seems to satisfy them, so I run out to my SUV. Hop in. Realize I've misplaced my cell phone. Go back in the club. It's not there." He ran his fingers through his hair in exasperation. "So I start heading over to the hotel and get caught in traffic. I think I moved ten feet in forty-five minutes. It took me another forty-five to get over to the right lane so I could ditch my SUV in a no parking zone, just down the block from the ongoing street repairs. I hop a couple barriers—"

Which explained the black grease smudges on his shirt, Holly mused.

"—and run the rest of the way to the hotel, where according to the maid who was cleaning down the hall, I just missed you. So I hoof it back to my SUV. Only to find it has already been ticketed and towed to an impound lot. Where it still sits."

Holly told herself this was not some sort of sign from

the universe that she had, once again, started down the wrong path and needed to do an immediate U-turn before she and Travis and their kids got really hurt. It was, instead, a shining example of Murphy's Law: Whatever can go wrong, will go wrong. Which meant they should have been braced for at least one calamity, if not all of them, given how much they'd both had riding on this.

"And your cell phone?" Holly questioned.

Travis grimaced. "I've got no idea where my Black-Berry is. Fortunately, there was a pay phone on the corner. I called Grady. He took pity on me, came and picked me up and brought me here."

Travis got points for showing up—eventually. But more were deducted for the information transfer to one of his very best male friends. Horrified, Holly flung her hand against her chest. "So Grady knows we were going to…" She blushed furiously.

Travis's scowl deepened at the inference. "He knows we were going to meet for lunch," he corrected. He gave her an irked look that let her know he would always protect her, and she should have known that without him saying so.

"And that I felt really bad about standing you up. So…" Travis let his smoldering gaze rove over her casually upswept hair and scalding cheeks before returning ever so slowly to her eyes. "Can I have a rain check?"

Holly paused, achingly aware of how much she wanted to say yes. Instead, her guard still up, she queried tersely, "When?"

Travis flashed her a mischievous grin, the picture of masculine relief. "Now," he said.

THE QUICK ACQUIESCENCE Travis had been hoping for did not materialize. Instead, Holly picked up her palette, dipped the tip of her paintbrush into the array of pinks, and went back to painting a delicate spray of flowers on the wall. "I can't, Travis. I've got to make up for the time I lost today."

He knew she usually worked through most of her lunch hour, as did he, in order to get home a little earlier in the evening, so she could spend more time with her twins before bed. However, that didn't mean they couldn't figure out *some* way to be together, particularly given how much they had both been looking forward to their tryst.

"This evening, then, after the twins are asleep," Travis persisted. He'd call Mrs. Ruley, or one of the other sitters they employed in emergencies.

Holly shot him a long-suffering glance. "We have the preschool holiday music program to attend."

"Oh. Right." Travis mentally berated himself for temporarily losing track of that. It made it sound as if he didn't care about the kids, and he did. "After then?" he continued with a pleading look. They still had the suite. He could have more room service sent up. It could still be a helluva romantic evening, if she would just give them a chance to follow through on their original plans to be together.

Holly's spine remained stiff. "I appreciate the thought." She switched to green, carefully stroking in a stem and leaves. "But we have to be honest with ourselves. This sneaking around in the middle of the day, trying to catch a little nooky, just isn't me. It's not you, either."

Put that crassly, an insulted Travis thought, it sure

wasn't. But then maybe that was the point of her sarcasm. Maybe she was trying to talk them both out of it. But her plan wasn't working on him. He had not changed his mind in the least. He still wanted to be with her, more than anything. It was up to him to persuade her that was the right course to take.

Travis placed his hands on her shoulders and forced her to look up at him. "Look, I know it was a disaster." He followed the curve of her shoulders, loving the soft womanly way she felt, hating the misery in her eyes. "But the next time will run smoothly. And even if it doesn't, you and I have four young children between us. We're used to improvising!"

"I know that." Her soft, pretty lips tightened in frustration, her expression far too nonchalant to be believed. "I also know we've both got way too much on our plates, as is, to make this work on even a semiregular basis. And frankly—" she paused to set her palette and brush down, then clamped a hand on the back of her neck, looking surprisingly jittery and ill at ease "—I just—" she shook her head, struggling to explain her dismay "—there was something almost *seamy* about the way it felt, heading for a hotel room in the middle of the day."

Travis became calmer as her emotions rose. "Had we actually hooked up and made love, that would not have been the case," he insisted. He would have treated her with the tenderness and care she deserved. Better, frankly, than anyone ever had.

Holly gave him a look that spoke volumes. Travis noted she was both more beautiful than he had ever realized, and more fragile. "Suppose we had met someone we knew in the lobby or on the elevator?" she challenged. "How do we explain? The potential for embarrassment is enormous!"

Travis admitted he didn't want anyone else guessing at his private affairs, either. The fact they'd felt they had to go to a hotel to achieve any real intimacy whatsoever wasn't good. "Then what do you suggest we do?" he asked, his own frustration rising. "You've already said you don't feel comfortable making love when all the kids are under the same roof, for obvious reasons. Last weekend demonstrated that they're too young for sleepovers anywhere but our own two houses. You don't want to go to a hotel…" His voice trailed off. He waited for her to make the next call, since she was the one coming up with all the excuses.

She shrugged as her natural wariness kicked in, and turned away from him. "That's just it. Maybe we shouldn't be doing this."

Travis watched her pace the nursery, hurt warring with the disappointment within him. He knew they weren't *in love* with each other, but he did love her, and he had been looking forward to feeling even closer to her. He couldn't believe, as potent as their first lovemaking encounter had been, that she would be nixing any further contact. He approached her, arms outstretched. "You don't mean that."

She held up a hand, refusing to let him take her in his arms. "I do. I had an hour to think about it while I was waiting for you to show up, and I realized that first and foremost I'm a mom." Deliberately, she kept her eyes on his. "If I was still married, still a wife, of course I'd be having sex on a regular basis. I'd be able to lock the bedroom door at night after my kids were asleep, and make love with my husband and feel great about it. But I'm not married. I'm a single mom with an example to set. Before we kissed…and my hormones got all stirred up again…I had successfully turned off that part of me. I was a happy celibate, Travis."

"So was I," he countered gruffly. "Then." Not now. Not knowing what they could have if only she'd meet him halfway!

"The point is marriage is not an option for us," she countered, looking just as determined as he felt.

The hell it wasn't, if that was what it took! "But maybe it should be," Travis blurted.

HOLLY STARED AT TRAVIS in astonishment. She'd thought the day could not get more surreal. She could not have been more wrong. She perched her hands on her hips. "You can't seriously be suggesting we get married just so we can conveniently have sex with each other!"

Undeterred, he continued impatiently, "Of course not. But we could get married because we have success-fully formed a very nice partnership over the past several years, we enjoy each other's company, our kids get along great, and we all love each other. As far as I'm concerned, those are very valid reasons for turning our situation into one big happy family."

That was all true and it was a very logical argument. "Except for one thing," she countered.

"And what's that?" he demanded.

"True love." Although she had grown used to an existence without it, she could not believe *he* would ever be happy without it.

Travis shrugged and continued to study her as if

trying to figure something out. Finally, he said, "We've each already had the big romance. Yours didn't work out. Mine ended prematurely. So—" he narrowed his eyes "—maybe we should do it differently this time. Base our union on friendship, shared goals, great sex and familial love."

Holly could be just as stubborn as he could, especially when he was being this exasperating. She looked away, her emotions in turmoil. "We can't do that," she said, wishing he didn't look so damn good, despite his disheveled state.

He swaggered closer. "Why not?"

A distracting shiver swept through her. What would it take to make this man realize that her difficulties in the romance department were not his problem? Holly stilled him with an equally presumptuous look. "Because one of us might find another big love, and then that person is going to want to pursue it."

An awkward silence fell. Holly noticed, to her disappointment, that Travis didn't deny the truth of her statement. He slid his gaze to the hollow of her throat, to her lips and then her eyes, all innocence once again. "I don't want to give up on us," he said finally.

"I don't, either," she said firmly, watching as he rocked back on his heels. "I'm just saying we should go back to the way things were between us."

TRAVIS HADN'T GIVEN UP on the two of them intimately connecting again, although he knew Holly assumed he had. He was just waiting for everything to cool down before he resumed his quest to make love to her again. And from there…who knew what would happen? He'd thrown out the idea of marriage as a way of making her comfortable with the sexual component of their relationship. And he'd meant what he said, too. He could see them getting married and blending their two families, having life roll along more smoothly than ever before.

In the meantime, he managed to get his SUV back, but had been forced to pay a steep fine and go to the impound lot to collect it. About a dozen problems had cropped up at the construction site in his absence, but he'd put all that off until tomorrow. This evening, as the six of them headed for the preschool show, all Travis wanted to focus on was the way it felt to have Holly and all the kids piled in his SUV, like the big happy family they still technically weren't.

While he drove, with the kids giggling in the back, Travis sneaked a peek at Holly in the passenger seat. She was wearing a white cashmere sweaterdress that hugged her slender frame, and white heels. Her golden-brown hair fell in a smooth, glossy line over her shoulders. A gold heart pendant nestled in the V of her dress, between her breasts. Her soft lips glistening with some sort of pink gloss, looked incredible, too. As if they were just begging to be kissed.

Even as the rest of her told him no.

The patient part of Travis knew he had to give her time.

He hoped when she thought about all they could have together, if given the chance, she would keep the idea of marriage firmly planted in the back of her mind.

This evening, however, he was happy just being with her and the kids. And his pride in his informal family intensified as he escorted them all inside the school. They looked so cute in their holiday clothes.

The kids were deposited at their classrooms, as per

preperformance instructions. Camera at the ready, Travis took his seat beside Holly at the end of one row. Picture taking was allowed, as long as the view of other parents wasn't obscured. It was his plan to slip out of his seat at the appropriate times and take photos from a station against the wall. And snag as much time with Holly as he could while they waited.

To his frustration, however, they had almost zero time to talk to each other. People kept stopping by to chat. At previous events, conversation had centered around the kids—theirs and everyone else's. Tonight, talk reverted to the previous week's news story involving the school, Santa, and one notoriously single dad in need of a wife....

To his and Holly's chagrin, everyone seemed to have a solution for his problem.

"Love to introduce you to someone you'd be perfect with...."

"Have you heard of Foreverlove.com? I bet one of their matchmakers could help you find just the woman you're looking for!"

I've already found her, Travis thought. *She just doesn't want to be married to me, even though marriage would solve everything.* Maybe his buddies were right. Maybe it was time to quit thinking about the risk of upsetting what they had, and stake a claim on the woman beside him.

"I heard you're one of the eligible men up for grabs Saturday evening," the preschool fund-raising chairman said to him.

Travis blinked. He had no clue what she was talking about.

Holly turned to give him a questioning look, and

suddenly, he had her full attention. Judging by the steely glint in her eyes, she was about as pleased with him now as she had been when he had shown up at Grady's, to explain standing her up.

He shrugged, letting her know he had no idea what the chairwoman had meant.

The loquacious woman jogged his memory. "The silent auction at the Kimball Museum? It's all over the news that you volunteered to be one of the successful, highly eligible men available for dates on New Year's Eve. The organizers of the fund-raiser for the Baptist Children's Home said they expect an evening with you to bring in some very big bucks! Anyway, congratulations on being asked to participate." The ebony-haired flirt flashed a mischievous smile and winked. "If I weren't married, I'd make a bid myself."

Holly watched the woman float off. "I just bet she would," Holly muttered under her breath.

Travis chuckled in amazement. "You sound jealous." Another first!

Holly harrumphed and didn't reply. A second later, the lights dimmed twice—the signal the program was about to start. Everyone still standing took their seats. And Holly and Travis's attention was diverted to the sweet sights and sounds of their children filing onto the stage in their holiday best.

"DON'T YOU HAVE WOMEN to be fending off or something?" Holly asked Travis sweetly the following morning, when he appeared on her doorstep after dropping all four kids off at preschool.

So she *was* jealous. Which could only mean one

thing, Travis thought in satisfaction. Her feelings were getting as out-of-control as his. Determined to set a few things straight—while they had a moment alone—he strolled on in without waiting for an invitation.

As he passed by her, he took in everything about her— the snug-fitting T-shirt and jeans that made the most of her slender frame. The loose updo that accentuated the graceful slope of her neck. The way the fragrant, womanly scent of her shampoo teased his senses.

Wondering when he would ever stop wanting to kiss her every time he saw her, and when she would admit to wanting to do the same, he studied her a good long time. Then murmured in a tone meant to rile her up even more, "The bidding is Saturday night."

Temper mingled with the resentment in her aquamarine eyes. Her tongue snaked out to wet her lips before she made a cantankerous face and said mockingly, "And the anticipation builds."

He grinned, appreciating the delicious pout of her lips almost as much as the emotion she couldn't hide. "You sound mad."

She tossed her head and glared at him. "I thought I was supposed to be jealous."

Unable to resist, he ribbed her a little more. "That, too."

She spun away. "I could care less!"

He had a fine view of her backside as she strode into the small room off the foyer that served as her studio and home office, and headed for the satchel of paints and brushes she took to every job. He watched as she pulled out empty plastic containers, tossed them in the trash can and replaced them with others in the same pastel hues.

"It's none of my business who you choose to squire

around on New Year's Eve this year! Especially for such a good cause."

He knew she was lying through her teeth to save face. "I'm glad you feel that way," he drawled.

She shrugged. "I'm glad you're glad."

Silence fell between them.

Travis knew he had to do what he'd come over there to do—end the tension between them and make peace. "For the record, I didn't know that was what I was volunteering for."

She exhaled slowly and kept her emotions veiled. "It really doesn't matter."

Aware she was watching him every bit as carefully as he was watching her, he told her the truth. "It does."

Holly worried her bottom lip with her teeth. "Why?"

He stepped closer. This time she didn't move away. "Because I don't want you to think I want to spend time with any woman but you."

Her lips pressed together in the stubborn pout he was beginning to know so well. Those lips he was determined to kiss again—and again. "We're not committed to each other," she reminded him.

And yet he still wanted her so badly, he ached.

Travis adjusted his stance to ease the pressure building at the front of his jeans. "Well, maybe we should be."

She tilted her head suspiciously. "Are you still talking about *marriage?*"

"I haven't given up on that," he told her stubbornly.

She resented the competitive edge to his voice. "This isn't a challenge to be won!"

Wasn't it? Travis couldn't think of anything—or

anyone—he had ever wanted more. He moved closer still, his heart filling with a depth of feeling he didn't expect. Yet, for her sake, he struggled to keep his tone casual. "A challenge? Like winning a damsel's heart?"

She flashed him a look that let him know he was pushing her too hard, too fast. "You've been watching too much bad TV."

"I haven't watched any," he told her gruffly, unable to stop himself when they had wasted so much time already. "And I don't need a script written by someone else to tell me what I want." He anchored his palms at her waist and watched her eyes widen.

"Travis!"

As he had figured, she had all her defenses up. That buffer crumbled the moment his mouth made contact with hers. She softened against him, allowing him to deepen the kiss. He nuzzled the side of her neck, finding the nerve endings just beneath her ear.

She moaned quietly. "I am supposed to be going to work."

He kissed her again and found her lips warm and sweet. "I'm sure Alexis and Grady will understand if the mural takes one more day."

She opened her mouth to the plundering pressure of his, and recklessly let herself yield. "That's not the point," she protested.

Travis had thought the first few times they had kissed had been amazing; their lovemaking wildly erotic. But that was nothing compared to how she felt in his arms right now—pure and hot and sensual beyond all reason. She kissed him with a yearning and an impatience that seemed to come straight from her soul. "You're right—

it's not," he whispered back, pausing to look into her eyes. "The point is I want you and you want me and Christmas is all about giving." He caught her lower lip between his teeth, worried it gently. "And what I want to give you is pleasure…."

She shivered in response, then released a shaky laugh. "Anyone ever tell you that you're relentless?"

Travis swung her into his arms and headed up the stairs. "In going after what I want? All the time," he confided, the intoxicating scent of her filling his senses. Gently, he lowered her onto her neatly made bed and dropped down to join her. "It's that kind of drive that's gotten me where I am today in business." He eased a hand beneath the hem of her T-shirt, gently caressing her ribs. "And what will get me where I want to be in my personal life, too."

He didn't say where that was, Holly noted, as they began to kiss again. And as they undressed with the same painstaking slowness as before, she wasn't sure she cared.

She had thought she could live the rest of her life without making love ever again. She had told herself that the love of her children and friends was enough. She didn't need any man to charge in and take command— in the bedroom or out. And she stuck to that easily, except when Travis was around. Then, it was impossible, especially when he kissed her and touched her and possessed her as if they had always been slated to be together. He made her feel as if the future was theirs for the taking. All she had to do was muster the courage to see where this fierce physical attraction between them led.

And that wasn't hard to do when his tongue was stroking hers, his hands were slipping beneath her, the powerful muscles of his chest were abrading her breasts. As he flattened her against him, she could feel the tingly heat spreading through her and she threw her whole heart into the steamy embrace. Morning sunlight streamed in through the blinds, bathing their bodies in a luminous glow. And still she couldn't get enough of him. The taste of his skin, the hardness of him, the heat.

Kisses poured out of them, one after another. Feelings built. And then there was no more waiting. Travis was parting her thighs with his knee, making sure she was as ready as he, and then they were one. Desire exploded in liquid, melting heat. She surged against him, moved with him, feeling sexier, more adventurous than she ever had in her life. The kisses stopped. Their eyes locked. She had never felt more beautiful than at that moment, seeing the admiration in his gaze. Never been more aware of the power one man and one woman together could feel. Never wanted anything to endure more.

And then he lowered his mouth and they kissed again, as if this and this alone would save them. And as they soared together to new heights, Holly knew Travis was right about one thing—what they had discovered in each other was a very special gift.

Afterward, he cuddled her close and said with distinctly male satisfaction, "Tell me you didn't enjoy that."

Pressed against him as she was, Holly reveled in the feel of warm smooth skin and firm muscle. He kissed her once more, slowly at first, then hotter, harder, deeper.

"Tell me you don't want to do it again."

She opened her mouth to the pressure of his, tangling her tongue with his, using the sweet suction of her lips and the roaming ministrations of her hands to drive him wild, too. "You know I can't."

She rocked against him, leaving him absolutely no doubt about what she wanted, and the best thing about it was that he wanted it, too. She took the lead. Travis surrendered until he could bear it no more. He rolled her over, captured her wrists in his hands and drew them above her head. She lay beneath him, captive to whatever he wanted—and what he wanted, he quickly proved, was her heart and soul. Again and again and again…

Chapter Ten

Neither Holly nor Travis made it into work that morning. But by noon they couldn't deny real life any longer. Mrs. Ruley and the four kids were due home from preschool any moment. The messages on Travis's cell phone were piling up. Holly had received a call from Alexis wanting to know if everything was okay, since she hadn't shown up to work on the mural, and another from a reporter wanting to know if Holly would care to comment on Travis's involvement in the silent auction at the Kimball Museum, since he wouldn't.

There was another message for both of them about the annual cookie swap at the preschool on Friday, before the students disbanded for the two-week holiday vacation. Both Travis and Holly were supposed to bring six dozen of their favorite Christmas cookies, and store-bought treats were discouraged. The faculty wanted this to be an experience for moms and dads and kids, all baking together.

And last but not least was a message on Holly's voice mail from Cliff.

It was the first time she had heard his voice since their

divorce was final, three years ago. She wasn't prepared for the cool familiarity of it.

"Holly—it's Cliff. Just wanted you to know that my flight arrives at DFW at 1:52 p.m. Saturday. I should be at your home by three, if all goes well. I'm not planning to stay that long—I'm spending the rest of the weekend with my old college roommate, Simon Armstrong. I imagine you remember him."

Holly did. Simon was an insurance executive now, unmarried the last time she had heard. He had always wanted kids. And had been furious with Cliff when he had abandoned her and the twins, asserting that one day Cliff would sorely regret what he had done.

It was interesting that Cliff would be staying with Simon. Had the friendship been rekindled now that Cliff was showing an interest in his sons? Had it been Simon Armstrong who encouraged or perhaps even prodded Cliff into making this visit?

Holly didn't know.

Cliff continued. "I wanted you to know that I am bringing two identical gifts the clerk at FAO Schwartz assured me were all the rage with three-year-old boys. I'll see you all Saturday."

"Everything okay?" Travis asked, coming to join her in the foyer.

She set her phone to replay the message. "You listen and tell me."

He did. When the recording had finished, he handed the phone back to her. "He's not planning to stay long."

"No kidding."

Travis wrapped a comforting arm around her shoulders and reeled her in close to his side. "That makes you angry."

"As well as hurt and disillusioned and heaven only knows what else." She paused, shook her head in silent remonstration. She ran her hand along the staircase banister, aware that Travis was ready to leave. But she needed him here, too, at least for a few minutes, and he was perfectly willing to stay and listen.

Holly swallowed and forced her gaze to his face. The understanding she saw in his dark eyes gave her the courage to put aside her self-imposed independence, and vent. "Cliff hasn't seen his kids in over three years now, because he hasn't cared to, and now suddenly he gets it in his head that he wants to take a gander at them, after all. So he's flying halfway across the country for a look-see. And then going right to another social engagement for the rest of the weekend! It's like the kids are some company Cliff is doing a prospective on to decide whether or not the bank should invest any time or money in it!" Tears stung her eyes as she continued bitterly, "Only Tucker and Tristan aren't some nonfeeling entity."

"You're damn right they're not," Travis said, looking as if he wanted to throttle Cliff for his selfishness, too.

Holly took a deep, enervating breath, glad Travis was there for her, because she needed his friendship, support, and yes, comfort, more than ever before. "And last but not least," she said, sliding her hand into his, "it really ticks me off that Cliff is willing to spend a lot more time reconnecting with his old college roommate than he is with his kids."

Travis inclined his head and squeezed her hand. When he spoke his voice was grim. "It certainly says something about Cliff's priorities."

"Doesn't it?" Holly felt her shoulders slump in defeat. How could she have thought the question of custody and visitation was all in the past? Even more telling, how could she protect her kids when Cliff had every right to see them? There were no laws that could force to him love his sons. Or make the twins feel as if they mattered to him, anywhere near as much as they mattered to Travis.

Travis pulled her in close again, shielding her with his warmth and his strength, even as he studied her compassionately. "Have the kids said anything more about their dad coming to see them, since you told them?"

Holly rested her head on Travis's shoulder. "Unfortunately, yes." Her hands worried the buttons on his shirt. "They were talking about it again last night before bed." She paused and slid her arms all the way around him, resting her face in the curve between his shoulder and neck. "I guess seeing the other dads in the audience at the school program made them aware that one day their daddy could be sitting in the audience, too."

Travis held her close. "Only you don't have any faith that Cliff ever will be." He kissed the top of her head and buried his face in her hair.

Holly reveled in the affection and tenderness that were so much a part of Travis. Finally, she lifted her head and confessed, "I can't explain—I just know Cliff. Once he decides something or someone is not worth his time or energy, he never goes back on that decision."

Travis's eyes narrowed thoughtfully. "But he is coming to see the kids. So even though he abandoned them once, and has stuck by that decision for the last three plus years…"

She sighed, seeing where this was going. "Maybe he does have some regret. Heaven knows he should, considering what he's given up, in cutting off all contact with his sons."

Travis shrugged and took the opposing view. "It might benefit the twins to have some relationship with him."

"Only if it's a loving, caring, nurturing one." Holly stipulated with a frown.

He realized that the situation was extremely complicated. "At some point the boys are going to want to know who their father is as a person," he warned Holly. "It might not happen until they hit adolescence, but from everything I've read on the subject, eventually they will want to know whatever they can about their father."

"And what if the only thing we have to tell them is that he abandoned them?" Holly cried. "Not once but twice! Or worse, that he's only seeing them at all because he wants to mend the rift with his old college roommate—who was furious with Cliff for ever deserting them in the first place." Briefly, Holly explained.

Travis shook his head as if to clear it. "First of all, why would Cliff go to all that trouble just to please Simon?"

That troubled Holly, too. "I don't know." She threw up her hands in frustration. "In terms of business, it wouldn't seem that Cliff would have anything to gain. Simon is an insurance executive and is based in Texas. Cliff works for an investment bank with an international presence." She gnawed on her lip. "Their friendship used to mean a lot to Cliff, when he and I were first married. But the two of them pretty much stopped speaking over Cliff's uncaring attitude toward the kids, after they were born."

Travis shrugged. "Maybe Cliff has realized that Simon was right all along, and wants to make amends."

Holly considered that. On the one hand, she couldn't see Cliff doing anything that didn't benefit him immensely. On the other, she knew that Cliff and Simon had once been extremely close, more like brothers than friends. So it was possible, she supposed, that Cliff had really missed the friendship. Although again, there was something about all this that just didn't ring true to her.

Travis caught her shoulders with his hands. "Are you going to be all right?"

She nodded and met his eyes with a searching gaze of her own. "I weathered the abandonment of my children by their father once. If after all this he deserts them again, I'll handle that, too. The difference is, on some level, this time my boys will know it's happening, too." And that was enough to break her heart all over again.

WEDNESDAY EVENING, JUST BEFORE suppertime, Holly got a message from Travis that he was running behind and would have to meet her later than expected, at the Carson Construction warehouse. After the backlog of work that had piled up for him the last thirty-six hours, Holly decided she would be surprised if he was able to get there at all to help her with the painting.

But that was okay, she told herself gamely, after the departing workers let her in and she settled down to sketch in first the control panel on the spaceship, and then the playhouse mural. She might not be able to finish in one six-hour stretch, as she had planned, without an equal amount of effort from Travis, but she was used to working alone.

Twenty minutes later, a door opened and closed, and purposeful footsteps sounded on the concrete floor. Holly turned to see Travis stride in. Her heart did a little happy dance in her chest. He was still dressed as he had been when he'd left her earlier in the day, in shirt, tie, dress pants and boots—attire suitable for his afternoon meeting with city officials. He carried paint-splattered jeans and a colorful work shirt, sweat socks and athletic shoes.

Without breaking stride, he came straight for her, took her in his arms and kissed her passionately. When they finally came up for air, her pulse was pounding and she tingled all over. He looked equally aroused and ready for action.

He stroked a hand through her hair and lamented in a low, humorous tone, "If only we didn't have so much work to do on these presents…"

"And so little time left to do it in," Holly murmured.

Travis kissed her again, with a mixture of obvious regret and tenderness. "We'll make up for it, I promise."

She didn't doubt that they would. If their lovemaking that morning had shown her anything, it was that she would always want him. And he her…

She no longer knew if just being friends with benefits was going to be enough. She still didn't want a marriage of convenience, but didn't want to invest this much of herself, emotionally, in their relationship and have no real ties to him.

It was going to be hard enough for her to watch him go out with another woman on New Year's Eve, for charity. She couldn't imagine what it would feel like if he ever did meet someone and feel for her what he'd once felt for his late wife.

Holly kept telling herself she would wish him well and let him go, because most of all, she wanted him to be happy. But she no longer knew if that was true, if she was that generous of a person, after all.

Oblivious to the complicated nature of her thoughts, Travis reached for the first couple of buttons on his shirt. "So where do you want me to start?" he asked her casually.

Knowing it would only entice her further to watch him change, she ducked back into the playhouse, just as a dress shirt sailed past the window and landed on the floor. The thud of his boots and the swish of his pants followed. "Concentrate," she told herself fiercely, as she penciled in the last of the chair rail that rimmed the interior.

She heard the rasp of clothing being drawn on as she drew a kitchen on one wall. A bedroom set on another. By the time she had worked back around to the already finished living room, Travis had stepped inside the six-foot-high domicile. He was too tall for the interior, so stooped over. "The girls are going to love this."

"The boys are going to love the spaceship." Determined to get this done, tonight if possible, she sized him up. "How are you at staying within the lines?"

His wicked smile said he inferred all kinds of things from that question. But when he answered he was definitely focusing on the task at hand. "I can do that," he told her cheerfully.

She showed him what color to paint where. While he filled in the background, she did the detail work. He was surprisingly adept with a paintbrush.

"No surprise there," Travis said when she complimented him. "I was going out on construction jobs with my dad by the time I was in school. At first, I was little more than an amusing sidekick, but over the years he taught me the basics of carpentry, painting, plumbing and electrical."

It felt good, working side by side with him. Especially on something that would mean so much to their kids, come Christmas morning. Trying hard not to notice how handsome Travis looked, even at the end of a long day, she asked, "How did your mom feel about that?"

He shrugged and hunkered down to get to a spot along the floor. As he moved, the soft, worn fabric of his jeans nicely gloved the taut muscles of his legs. "Mom wanted me to go into business with Dad when I grew up," he related. "She thought he worked too hard, being a solo operator, and she was right. He died of a stress-induced heart attack when he was fifty. My mom followed a couple years later, with an aneurysm."

Holly gave Travis a sympathetic glance and squeezed his hand. She knew what it was to lose a parent. She had lost both her parents in an automobile accident when she was twenty-two.

"Anyway, I took over his company and started expanding it almost right away, doing all the things Dad never felt comfortable doing—hiring employees, taking on multiple jobs, going after ever bigger, more lucrative projects. That's how I met Grady and the guys." Travis smiled, reflecting. "They were all busy building their businesses, too."

She couldn't help but admire them for it. "You have all succeeded handsomely."

Travis beamed. "In business—absolutely." He regarded her steadily. "In my personal life, there are still goals I want to achieve."

Before Holly had a chance to ask what he meant by that, the cell phone on his belt went off. He looked at the screen, put down his paintbrush and stepped outside the playhouse. "Sorry. I have to take this," he said over his shoulder.

"Hey, Nate. It's definitely going to be competitive," she heard him say. "We just have to make sure our numbers beat theirs….shear off every penny without sacrificing one iota of quality, which is where you and your guys come in… Tomorrow morning, first thing. Thanks, buddy."

Holly shifted over to the spaceship and began painting in dials and gages on the control panel. "Things heating up with the opera project?" she asked when he rejoined her.

"A little." He picked up a brush and began painting some of the trim there. "Although they are a long way from deciding what will be built and who will get the job, the steering committee for the project wants to see some unoffical proposals from all the firms in contention, along with cost projections, so they can set realistic fund-raising goals. That's what the meeting at the Cattleman's Club was about yesterday."

"Sounds high-pressure," Holly remarked.

"You've got that right." Travis sighed anxiously. "None of it is due until February, but the guys and I all want to get a jump on it. Whoever has the best ideas out of the gate will have a big advantage over everyone else when the actual bidding process happens next summer. Assuming, of course, the organizers are able to get the funds they need."

Holly appreciated Travis's gung ho attitude and spirited work ethic. "You really like competing, don't you?"

"Gets my blood pumping every time. Especially in situations like this, when one of the contenders is behaving unethically."

"By trashing you to the client."

Travis nodded. "Then it becomes as much of a moral battle as a business one. And you know me, I always want the good guys to win, justice to be had, etc."

"Your strong sense of right and wrong is one of the things I've always liked about you," Holly said, playfully winding her arms about his neck. "I also admire your ability to quickly and easily adjust to parameters of every situation in order to stay competitive." He was tough and fiercely determined to get what he wanted, in business, and in his personal life. That made him a hard person to go up against. Fortunately, the two of them had always been on the same page.

"It's good to know I'm appreciated." Travis kissed her tenderly, until both knew if they continued down this path, the work would never get done. He drew back. "So back to the task at hand?"

Holly withdrew reluctantly, too. With Christmas only days away now, they had no choice but to stay focused on what mattered, and right now that was giving the kids their happiest Christmas ever. "You bet."

"DADDY," MIA EXCLAIMED, as Travis tucked her into bed at Holly's house Thursday evening, "this was the mostest fun ever!"

Travis thought so, too. He and Holly and their kids had all been close before, but this holiday season had intensified that intimacy to the point he knew he didn't ever want to go back to being just friends and neighbors. He wanted them to be this close to each other all the time.

He knew that probably wouldn't be a problem as long as there was no other man in Holly's life. But with her ex showing up in less than forty-eight hours, Travis wasn't as certain about her allegiance to him as he had been. It wasn't that he thought Holly had feelings for Cliff. He was fairly certain that was not the case. It was her devotion to her kids, and her wanting to do what was best for Tucker and Tristan, that might lead her back to her ex. Certainly, he'd seen it happen before....

"I can't wait to show our teachers all the cookies we baked tonight!" Sophie agreed.

"They taste awesome!" Tucker said with a yawn.

Tristan rubbed his eyes sleepily. "Especially the ones with chocolate kisses in the middle!"

Travis leaned down to kiss and hug each child in turn. Holly did the same. The feel of familial love in the room intensified. "You go to sleep now," Holly told the kids. "Tomorrow is a school day. The last one before vacation."

"'Night," the kids mumbled.

Travis followed Holly out of the twins' room, where all four children were now bedded down for the night. She shut the door. Together, they returned to the kitchen.

"I can't believe this mess," Holly murmured, looking overwhelmed by the extensive cleanup that lay ahead of them. Confectioner's sugar and frosting seemed to be everywhere, as were a myriad of crumbs and cookie cutters, bowls, spoons, and baking pans.

Travis knew they would handle this the way they

handled every difficulty that came their way—with speed and efficiency.

In the meantime, he had a goal of his own to achieve. He peered at her closely. "I think you've got something in your hair."

"What?"

"Stand over here." He positioned her a little to the left, with her back to the counter. He tucked a hand beneath her chin as he inspected the golden-brown strands covering one ear. "Now, look up."

Perplexed, Holly did. And then she chuckled. "Mistletoe."

"By golly, you're right." Travis grinned mischievously. "It is! And you know what that means. By custom, men kiss the women standing under it."

Holly opened her mouth and his lips covered hers. Heat and gentleness combined with the taste of sweet confection and woman. And although Travis knew that Holly probably felt this was the last thing they should be doing tonight, he didn't care. He wanted her. She wanted him. It had been too long since either of them had felt this happy or alive. So, if a little kiss here and there—actually a lot of stolen kisses here and there— were what it took to keep the flame alive, then—

"Mommy?" Tucker interrupted.

"Whatcha doin?" Tristan inquired.

"We need water," Sophie said.

"Can we have more cookies?" Mia asked.

Holly unhooked her arms from around Travis's neck and stepped back.

"We were kissing underneath the mistletoe," Travis explained.

Sophie's tiny brows furrowed as she observed them, "When grown-ups kiss all the time, it means they are getting married. Daddy, are you and Holly getting married? Because if you do, then she would be our mommy for real, wouldn't she?"

Travis and Holly exchanged looks again. For the first time that he could remember, both of them were speechless.

"But that can't happen," Tucker interjected, eager to put his two cents in as well. "Remember?"

Tristan propped his hands on his pajama-clad hips. "That's right. We already got a daddy and he's coming to see us on Saturday!"

"So the evening ended, just like that?" Grady asked the next morning, after Travis had brought his friends up to speed.

Travis helped himself to one of the breakfast burritos in the center of the conference table, where the guys had gathered to check the status on One Trinity River Place and brainstorm on how to land their next big project—the proposed opera hall.

Travis had told them he'd decided to follow their advice and pursue Holly. He now readily admitted to himself he wanted her long term. And he was equally certain, if she were honest, she wanted him the same way, too.

The trouble was, she kept letting every little stumbling block get in the way of that happening.

One minute she'd be kissing him and making love with him like there was no tomorrow. The next, she'd be telling him they had to cool it, and showing him the door....

Aware that his friends were waiting for the continuation of the story of last night's events, Travis related, "Holly said the kids were too wound up to be able to sleep in the same room last night, which was probably true, since they all had way too much sugar during the cookie-making extravaganza. So she sent me home with the girls, put her boys to bed and handled the clean-up alone."

Dan shook his head. "You're right—that is a bad sign. Especially if the kitchen was as much of an unholy mess as you said."

"It was. It definitely was."

Jack popped open his coffee. "Do you think she might have feelings for Cliff?"

Travis's gut clenched. "She says she doesn't."

"Yeah, but she hasn't seen him again yet, either," said Jack, whose ex-wife had run off with a previous husband, leaving him and their infant daughter behind.

Nate commented, "I think she's ticked off about the idea of you spending New Year's Eve with a woman who will have paid for the pleasure of your company."

That hadn't occurred to Travis. The silent auction at the Kimball was the following evening.

"You ask me, you got yourself in a heap of trouble saying yes to that," Nate continued, with the authority of the only lifelong bachelor in the group, and hence, the one with the most dating experience.

Grady kicked back in his chair with a take-out serving of hash brown potato cakes. "I agree. It may be for a good cause, but it's a bad move for any guy trying to land himself a bride."

Travis held up a warning hand. "I never said I was trying to get her to marry me." At least not in the traditional sense.

Dan grinned. "You will," he predicted. "Just watch."

Judging by the looks on their faces, everyone else in the room seemed to agree.

"In the meantime," Jack said with a companionable nudge, "I've got a thought on how you should handle this whole New Year's Eve dilemma."

Travis didn't deny the bachelor auction was a problem. But first, they had an even bigger obstacle looming.

"ARE YOU OKAY?" TRAVIS ASKED Holly, as they stood in her formal living room, Saturday afternoon.

In the adjacent kitchen, Tucker and Tristan were dressed in button up shirts, V-necked sweater vests, corduroy pants and brown leather shoes. Their blond hair was combed, teeth brushed, faces washed. They sat side by side at the kitchen table, diligently drawing and coloring Christmas pictures for their daddy. Their favorite Christmas music played softly on the portable stereo, adding to the aura of tranquility.

Holly was wearing black slacks and a matching turtleneck sweater. Outwardly, she knew she looked good. Inside, she felt sick.

"You're awfully pale," Travis noted gently.

Glad he had agreed to be there with her to lend moral support, Holly pretended an ease she couldn't begin to really feel. "I'm fine." She wanted to believe so, anyway.

They heard a car pull up outside.

Holly tensed, despite herself. She drew a deep breath and headed for the foyer. Travis was right behind her. Through the transom windows beside her front door, she could see Cliff stepping out of a chauffeured limousine, two elaborately wrapped presents in hand.

Her ex looked just as he had the last time she had seen him. Polished, professional, slickly urbane. He spoke to the driver, who apparently intended to spend the time parked at her front curb, then headed up the walk.

Holly opened the door. Made introductions. Travis and Cliff sized each other up, neither apparently liking what he saw.

The tension in the foyer grew thicker. "The boys?" Cliff asked.

"Are waiting to meet you." Heart thudding uncomfortably in her chest, Holly led the way to the kitchen.

Tristan and Tucker looked up.

At such close proximity, it was apparent they were in the same room with their biological father. In addition to their fair hair and skin, there was a certain similarity of eyebrow, the jut of their chins, the angle of their cheeks and the shape of their ears.

"I see you are coloring," Cliff said.

The boys—suddenly speechless—ducked their heads and nodded.

Cliff sat down and Holly served the coffee.

Travis made himself as innocuous as a fly on the wall.

Cliff offered the presents to the boys. They opened them with none of their usual enthusiasm, but seemed happy enough with their miniature truck and car sets, once they were out of the packaging.

"Are you going to be here for Christmas?" Tucker asked, racing a dump truck on the table in front of him.

Tristan mimicked his brother's play. "Because our bestest friends want a mommy for Christmas. And we told them we already had a daddy," he said. He looked up at Cliff intently. "So are you going to be here?"

"In Texas?" Cliff smiled, seemingly unaware he was being put to the test by his sons. "No. I already have plans to go skiing in Zurich over the holidays, before I start work again on January second."

The boys stared at him uncomprehendingly, then put their new toys aside and went back to coloring solemnly.

The conversation continued a few more minutes.

Finally, Cliff stood, looking as if he had already tired of the effort to play daddy. "I think I've seen what I need to," he told Holly surreptitiously.

What in heaven's name did that mean? she wondered, more anxious than ever. And angry, too, that this cold, heartless man had the potential to come back into their lives and turn their world upside down, on what seemed to be a whim.

Cliff inhaled deeply, looking all the more serious. "I want to think about this, talk to the people close to me, and then get back to you via my attorney on Monday."

And I'd like you to stop acting like you get to come in here and call all the shots, Holly thought.

Travis loomed at Holly's side. Like an Old West cowboy riding to the rescue of his lady, he clapped an implacable hand on Cliff's shoulder and steered the investment banker into the foyer. "Why don't you just tell Holly what you have in mind now?" he growled.

Yes, Holly thought. *I'd like to know if I need a lawyer, too.*

Cliff looked Travis up and down. "I'm sure you mean well," he said, his resentment obvious.

Oh, Lord, Holly thought. *Please don't go there. This is Texas, after all.* Travis was not a person to suffer fools or stand by and watch anyone he cared about get hurt.

"No offense, but what I tell Holly—and when—is my decision. And mine alone. And before I make my formal offer," Cliff stated coolly, "it's only good business to make sure everything is in perfect order. So, Holly. Monday at noon? Let's meet at my attorney's office."

"THAT WENT WELL," HOLLY remarked with a roll of her eyes after Cliff had departed.

Travis stood, watching Cliff's limo pull away from the curb. Every inch of him seemed primed and ready for battle. He turned to her, exuding the combination of masculine strength and fearlessness she loved.

With a rueful slant of his lips, he remarked, "I've got to tell you—I'm not usually a punch-somebody-out type of guy. But just now, I was severely tempted."

"Then that makes two of us," Holly said, trembling with a mixture of anger and fear. She could live to be a hundred and she would never understand how someone could be so insensitive!

In tandem, she and Travis shot a look into the kitchen. The twins were still coloring. Still unusually quiet.

Things looked normal, on the outside.

Holly couldn't help but wonder what the boys were feeling on the inside.

Certainly, there had been no instant rapport between Cliff and his sons. So if that was what he was looking for...

"It's going to be okay," Travis told her, rubbing his hand up and down her spine.

Holly gave in to the soothing ministrations, and rested her head on his shoulder. "I wish Cliff had just told me now what he has in mind," she said with a sigh. Now she had to wait the whole damn weekend to find out.

"It doesn't matter," Travis said firmly, as his hand stilled.

Holly looked up and their gazes locked.

"Together," Travis promised, with the tenderness and compassion she had come to rely on more and more each day. "We'll handle whatever comes our way."

Chapter Eleven

"Go with me tonight," Travis said, half an hour later, when talk had turned to plans for the rest of the day. Holly's Saturday night loomed like the miserable experience it was destined to be. Not because she didn't enjoy a quiet night alone, but this evening, the prospect of watching TV or unwinding in a relaxing bubble bath with a glass of wine held little appeal. Probably because she would be thinking of Travis, and the fervent bidding likely to be taking place for a date with him on New Year's Eve.

She couldn't blame the women interested in him.

The TV coverage of his daughter's quest for a mommy had been heartrending. Everyone in Fort Worth who'd heard the story was hoping Travis would find the wife he needed, and the mommy his little girls were dreaming about. Holly was hoping, too, at least in theory.

Reality was a little tougher to swallow.

Before they'd made love, she had thought she would be okay if he ever fell in love again. Most of all, she wanted him—and his two little girls—to be happy.

Now, she wasn't sure.

She only knew she wasn't magnanimous enough to stand around idly while Travis was bid on by throngs of amorous women.

Aware that he was waiting for her answer, she lifted a shoulder in a shrug. With difficulty, she put on her best poker face and looked Travis in the eye. "I'm not sure it's appropriate to take a date to an event like that," she told him matter-of-factly

He grinned, as if sensing she was nowhere near that cool inside. He shot her an unexpectedly flirtatious glance, then murmured, "Probably not, if it was strictly a bachelor auction sort of deal. But they're going to be bidding on all sorts of great stuff. Everything from dinners out to authentic lithographs of early Fort Worth. You might see something that would catch your fancy."

Like you? Holly thought wistfully to herself. The truth was, she didn't know what she would have done that afternoon when Cliff visited, had Travis not been there. She didn't know what she was going to do at Martin Shield's office on Monday, either, since she had no idea what was going to happen then, but she had promised herself she wouldn't spend the weekend brooding about it. So the two of them had joined forces, asking Mrs. Ruley if she would bring Travis's girls over to Holly's before she left. As soon as they had arrived, Holly and Travis had brought out the building blocks, wooden train set and miniature play sets and spread them out on the family room floor. All four kids were busy building their own Christmas village, complete with animal hospital, fire station, candy store, nursery school and family home. It was shaping up to be quite elaborate, and would keep them busy for some time.

Meanwhile, Holly was working on preparing several days' worth of dinners for her freezer and fridge, while Travis hung out and kept her company. "You'd be supporting a great cause…and be keeping me from having to show up to face all those women alone," he said, continuing his pitch for the silent auction.

She couldn't help laughing at his droll tone. He might complain sometimes about having to go out, but once there, he was always able to enjoy himself in a social setting.

"Who knows?" Travis watched her trim some string beans. "You might even find a great Christmas present for someone, if you haven't finished your shopping yet."

"Actually—" Holly put a pan with water on the stove "—I…haven't got anything for you yet." Not that she hadn't tried. Everything just felt either too impersonal or too intimate. Nothing she had looked at had been just right.

"You see?" Travis sat on the stool opposite her and wordlessly took over the task of trimming the rest of the beans. "I bet they have power tools and all sorts of things."

Aware she wanted nothing more than to kiss him again, right then and there, Holly sent her glance heavenward. She went to the fridge and got out the ingredients for her next dish. "I'm not buying you a power tool. You have more than enough of those. You own a construction company, for Pete's sake."

Travis grinned in a way that let her know he had been trying to get a reaction from her. "A shaving kit, then," he prodded mischievously.

Holly ran a hand over his exceptionally smooth jaw.

His skin was warm and taut as he briefly turned his lips into the center of her palm, surreptitiously delivering a kiss she felt all the way down to her toes.

She began to tingle all over. Christmas was definitely coming early this year, she thought. And they had four kids in plain view in the next room.

She glided away, to retrieve a big, stainless steel mixing bowl. "You don't seem to have any problems in the shaving department, either," she chided him before placing onion, green pepper and celery into the food processor for a quick chop. "So whatever kind of razor you're using…" She went back to the mixing bowl.

Travis worked slowly and precisely on the green beans. He gave her another slow once-over that made her feel as if he was making love to her all over again. "Triple-bladed extra platinum blade with a precision swivel head, and gel shaving cream."

"Well, it's doing a fine job," Holly stated.

He grinned and handed her the beans. "I'll be sure and let the manufacturer know you approve."

Holly put them on the stove to steam.

While Travis watched, she added bread crumbs, beaten eggs, ground turkey, diced tomatoes, salt and pepper, and the chopped vegetables to the bowl, then stirred it all together, and patted it into two loaves. One looked like a Christmas tree, the other a sleigh.

"The kids are going to love this," he said, as she slid them into the oven to bake.

Holly sighed, stripped off the food prep gloves she'd used to mix the meat, and tossed them into the trash. "Well, after all this effort, I sure hope so." She went to the sink to wash her hands.

Travis joined her, his shoulder touching hers, their fingers brushing beneath the stream. "Trust me, you have nothing to worry about." He winked.

He even made cooking dinner sexy, Holly realized with a wistful sigh. Which was part of the problem. She had a lot to get done here in a short amount of time. She plucked a sack of potatoes out of the pantry and carried them back to the sink, inclined her head and gave him a telling look. "You're getting me off track here."

He stepped back to give her room to work, but not so far he couldn't see every little thing she was doing. "Just as I was hoping." He flashed her another devil-may-care grin.

Figuring as long as he was standing there, he might as well make himself useful, she handed him a potato peeler, while she peeled with the utility knife. "Stop stalling, Travis. What do you want for Christmas?"

He gazed into her eyes. "Besides you?"

Unable to maintain eye contact without thinking about making love to him again, she dropped her glance to the strong column of his throat and the crisp, curling hair visible in the open V of his button-down cotton shirt. He smelled so good. His body was just so big and warm and strong. "I'm serious, Travis."

He quirked a brow at the increasingly pink contours of her face, seeming to know intuitively what she was thinking and feeling. "So was I."

Silence fell between them. Holly reminded herself about the auction, and the fact that although Travis loved her and desired her, he wasn't *in love* with her. And while she might be persuaded to settle for less, especially if "less" felt this good all the time, Travis would never be happy with that. He deserved more.

Hanging on to her resolve with everything she had, Holly stipulated, "I'm talking about a present I can buy." She really wanted a hint about what to get for him! This year, especially, she wanted her gift to him to be right.

But Travis, it seemed, wasn't the least bit interested in receiving. His lips curved into a sexy grin. "Ladies first. What can *I* get for you?"

More time…with you, Holly thought as she grabbed the dough she'd had rising and began on the cinnamon rolls. *Just lots and lots of time….*

But she couldn't say that without putting him on the spot. So she shrugged, and said, "I don't know."

Travis watched her prepare the dough, roll it into a long log and then slice it into rounds. "You see?" As at home in her kitchen as his own, he got out two glasses and filled them with ice and lemonade from the fridge. "Not so easy, is it?"

Holly arranged the cinnamon rolls in a glass baking dish and covered them loosely with plastic wrap. She set them in a warm place, next to the stove to rise. In need of a break, and a little fresh air, she stepped outside onto the patio, then turned to Travis, who had followed. Over his shoulder, through the glass, she could see all four kids, still busily working on erecting their Christmas village.

Glad for this time together with him, in the brisk December air, with the sun peeking through the clouds, she sipped her lemonade.

Travis gave her a confident look. "What was the best gift you ever had?"

FOR A LONG MOMENT, Travis thought Holly wasn't going to answer him. Not because she didn't know, but because she was wary of getting too close to him too fast, of letting sexual intimacy lead to an even greater emotional intimacy. Although she'd sworn off romantic love, he was finally ready for that kind of commitment. The question was, how was he going to get the two of them on the same page without her feeling pressured or backed into a corner, in the way that her ex was currently trying to do? Travis knew they could wait. But he also knew how short life could be, and that made him impatient.

Holly looked over at him, as if in awe of how good it felt to simply hang out this way. "In my entire life?"

He nodded.

She sank down on a cushioned wicker love seat and drew him down beside her. He settled in happily, and when he rested an arm across the back of the seat, she let her head fall back against it. She sipped her lemonade and said, "When I was a senior in high school, my parents gave me the money I needed to take a trip to Paris with my art class. That was pretty incredible."

Travis could imagine Holly there, then and now. He made a mental note to honeymoon there, when the time came. He buried his face in the fragrant softness of her hair. "What was the best gift you ever gave?"

She smiled as he nuzzled her temple, pressed another kiss on her brow, and snuggled closer. "I threw my parents a surprise anniversary party. Invited everyone they knew." She glowed at the memory. "They were really happy."

Travis stretched his legs out next to hers. The side of his thigh pressed into hers. The contact was warm and familiar, and he thought about kissing her again. "Your parents had a good marriage?"

"Oh, yes."

"So did my folks," he said softly.

Briefly, wistfulness lit her eyes. "I wish my marriage had lived up to the same standard."

"Your next one will," Travis told her.

She studied him, a wry smile tugging at her lips. "You seem so sure."

He tapped her playfully on the tip of her nose. "That's because I know you. And you deserve only the best." He paused to kiss her lips, sweetly and tenderly. "And the next time around, you'll get it."

She set both their empty glasses on a table, then turned back and snuggled closer, hope shining in her pretty aquamarine eyes. "This is one time I hope you know what you're talking about."

"I do. But we digress." He stroked a hand over her hair, aware how frequent moments like this could be if only they really joined forces and lived under the same roof. "What *can* I get you for Christmas?"

She relaxed even more into the curve of his body, looked deep into his eyes. "Anything you give me will be wonderful."

Travis thought about his failure to please Diana in that regard, how often she'd taken his presents back to exchange them for something she really wanted. He didn't want to make the same mistakes with Holly. "You say that now," he said, worrying out loud.

"I mean it. Really, I do. You have exquisite taste. And a kind heart. And wonderful common sense."

And A pluses in every category women looked for in

a man, except one, Travis thought drily. "And no talent whatsoever in the kitchen." Which could be, he realized belatedly, a reason she wouldn't want to marry him. Because she felt if she did, she would either have to shoulder the cooking alone, or worse, share the task with him and eat the kind of premade fare he could serve up. Neither option was very palatable.

"Only because you haven't learned how to cook anything that doesn't come in a box or can. Once you put a little time in, I have no doubt you'll be as good at that as you are at everything else."

"Then that's what I want for Christmas," Travis said, determined to be as competitive as possible in every realm.

Holly sat up straight and blinked in surprise. "What?"

"I want cooking lessons—from you."

AT FIRST, HOLLY DIDN'T think Travis was serious. But as soon as she realized he was, it put a whole new spin on things.

"And I want something else, too," he continued, as the two of them collected their glasses and went back inside, just in time to hear the oven timer go off. "I want you to go to the silent auction with me tonight."

Holly sighed. She should have known that they would eventually get back around to discussing the auction. After all, once Travis made his mind up that he wanted something, he was relentless in going after it.

"I'll make a deal with you," she said finally, appreciating how handsome and right Travis looked in her kitchen, being such an integral part of her life. "I'll attend the silent auction with you tonight if you and your kids agree to spend tomorrow with me and my kids at the mall."

"Shopping?" It was Travis's turn to look pained. "But I suppose one sacrifice deserves another," he quipped. Before she could speak, he pulled her beneath the mistletoe he had hung in her kitchen and kissed her soundly.

This time when their kids looked over and caught them, they merely smiled. The children were getting as used to his displays of affection as she was, Holly realized.

"So…" He let her go, bringing the conversation back to the original topic. "We have a deal."

Because the evening was a black tie affair, Holly and Travis had dinner together at her house, quickly dispensed with the dishes and soon parted company. Knowing it would take her a lot longer to get ready than him, he took all four kids over to his place, to await the return of Mrs. Ruley.

Feeling a mixture of excitement she didn't expect— and nerves because this was as close to a "date" as anything they'd done yet—Holly went upstairs and wandered to the back of her walk-in closet. There, on hangers, were a dozen gowns she hadn't worn since she had become pregnant with the twins.

Fortunately, her tastes ran to the simple and classic, so it wasn't hard to pick out a floor-length, black satin gown with a white satin bodice and Empire waist that would be perfect for the gala at the Kimball Museum. Delicate white-and-black jewelry, a warm black evening wrap and black stiletto heels completed the ensemble.

Enjoying the rare time to herself, Holly soaked in a luxurious bubble bath and spent as much time as she wanted applying her makeup. She put her hair up in an elegant twist, spritzed on her favorite perfume and then headed next door to join the others.

Travis was waiting, in the requisite black tuxedo and pleated white shirt. Christmas music was playing softly in the background. All four children were clad in their pajamas, lying around the base of the Christmas tree. Hands folded behind their heads, they were all studying the decorations and the sparkling lights, with sweet, dreamy expressions on their faces.

"How many more days until Christmas, Mommy?" Tucker asked.

Realizing this was the family they could have if she and Travis joined forces, the way he wanted, Holly knelt down near to the children. "Not counting today, four until Christmas Eve."

Sophie yawned. "I sure wish Santa could bring me and Mia a mommy. If he did, I bet she'd look just like you, like a pretty princess."

Seeing an opening, as well as a way to change the subject, Holly said gently, "Christmas isn't just about receiving gifts. It's about giving, too."

Travis nodded. "That's why we're taking you shopping tomorrow. So you can get gifts for the people you love."

"Like you and Holly and Mrs. Ruley," Tristan said.

"And each other." Holly bent to kiss and hug each child in turn.

"It's going to be fun, isn't it, Daddy?" Mia said, as Travis did the same.

They straightened just as the doorbell rang and Mrs. Ruley arrived. "Almost as fun as my evening with Holly tonight," Travis promised with a cheerful wink.

TALK ABOUT SPEAKING TOO soon, Holly lamented silently, two excruciatingly long hours later. It wasn't that there wasn't a lot to look at—and bid on—because there was. Gifts, large and small, abounded. There were eclectic and traditional choices. There were also dozens of people, some of whom she knew and many others she was enjoying meeting. The problem was the one person she would have liked to have spent more time with, the one person she had her heart set on, was strictly out of bounds to her. A fact noted by Alexis McCabe.

With a matchmaker's glint in her eyes, Grady's wife noted with sympathy, "Can't get near him, either, hmm?"

To the point, Holly mused, she was beginning to feel as if she had about as much Christmas spirit as The Grinch. "The news crews greeted Travis getting out of the car," she told her friend. "I got pushed aside in the crush and came on in. As soon as he entered, he was wrangled to go stand with the other men being auctioned for dates and then was formally introduced to the crowd. After that, they had to pose for pictures for all the local news outlets. As soon as that ended, the real stampede began."

Alexis looked over at the area where the silent auction was being conducted. Elegantly clad guests crowded the various exhibits, studying what was available, pausing to write down their bids and the secret ID numbers they had been assigned upon entering. Attached to every display was a sheet of paper where guests wrote down their bids, upping the amount of the previous one. The eligible men had been assigned booths where their photos and bios were displayed. All of them were also surrounded by female admirers, but Travis was literally swamped by women queuing up to talk to him. Organizers had been required to add additional pages to accommodate all the bids being placed for the New Year's Eve date with him.

"From what I understand, because of the thing with Sophie and Mia and their wish for a mommy, Travis is deemed the most truly marriageable man here," Alexis stated.

And probably the most eligible, if "sexy" was the only criteria, Holly thought, helping herself to a stuffed shrimp from the buffet table. "I know I shouldn't complain." She did her best to quash a beleaguered sigh. "It's for a good cause."

When it came to matters of the heart, Alexis was all about truth-telling. "Of course you should protest!" She eyed the buffet with the ravenous appetite of a pregnant woman, finally settling on the puff pastry stuffed with spinach, and artichoke dip. "Seeing the man you're interested in up for grabs has to be torture! If Grady were on the auction block, I'd be out of my mind with misery," she lamented softly.

That about covered it, Holly thought, unable to help but think how debonair Travis looked in his tux. In fact, he looked so spectacular tonight, he could give James Bond a run for his money. She turned back to the savvy matchmaker. "There's a slight difference—you and Grady are married."

Alexis shrugged and helped herself to another puff pastry, this one stuffed with chicken and cream cheese. "Given the breadth and depth of your arrangement with your next-door neighbor, it's about the same thing." She studied Holly with shrewd eyes. "Did you place a bid?"

"I thought about it," she confessed.

"And?"

Holly winced. "With bids starting at one hundred dollars and going into the steep four figures already? It's not practical." Especially when she might have to pay a lawyer soon to help resolve whatever was happening with Cliff.

Alexis consoled her with a pat on the arm. "Oh, well, it's only one night. And an arranged engagement for charity, at that. How fabulous could the date be?"

Alexis was right, Holly thought, as she noticed a notoriously sexy oil heiress taking sole command of Travis's attention. He was doing this out of the goodness of his heart. It should definitely not be a big deal. So why did it matter so much? Holly wondered in dismay.

"AT WHAT POINT DID you stop speaking to me?" Travis asked with a frown.

Holly turned her glance toward the street, and away from the man in the driver's seat, as they entered the subdivision where they lived. The houses were lit with festive lights, wreaths were on every door, Christmas trees prominently displayed. Travis even had her favorite orchestral Christmas music playing in his SUV. Yet Holly had never felt less yuletide spirit. Never felt less like giving or receiving.

She did her best to keep her heart on guard. "I don't think I did." All she wanted was for this travesty of a date to end.

"We're driving home and you're not talking to me. It's sort of the same thing." Smug male confidence radiated from him.

But then, why not? Holly thought. He'd spent the

entire night having his ego bolstered by a parade of beautiful, available women.

Women who might one day make him feel what he'd felt for Diana—what he clearly did not feel for Holly. The truth was, they had started out as friends and probably would never be able to move beyond that.

Aware that he was waiting for some explanation, she said finally, "It was a long evening, a long day."

He nodded. "And you're jealous."

Okay, that hit her where it hurt. For both their sakes, she pretended otherwise. "Can't stop flattering yourself, can you, Mr. Eligible Bachelor?"

Travis grinned at her wry tone, pulled into her driveway instead of his, and cut the motor. At his home, the lights were out, except for the front porch and foyer. Presumably, because it was after midnight, all their kids and Mrs. Ruley were already asleep.

Travis stepped out of the car. "I'll walk you inside."

Holly felt a fluttering deep within her. She lifted a hand and stopped him from coming closer. "As I said, it's late."

He paused to let his gaze drift slowly over her. "And we still need to talk."

"About?"

"Who won a date with me."

Holly knew the number of the bidder by heart; she just didn't know the identity, since all that information was privy only to the event organizers in order to protect everyone's privacy. Holly hoped it wasn't the rich young woman with the reputation of a sexual barracuda, but if it was, she couldn't do anything about that, either. "I really don't think I want to know that," she replied in a saccharine tone.

He arched a mocking brow. "Sure?"

"Very!"

Grinning at her all too clear enunciation, he watched her unlock the door, and followed her inside. "Is this our first fight?"

Holly dropped her evening wrap onto the console in the hall, set her purse on top of it.

The sleeveless, strapless gown that had been perfect for an evening at the museum now left her feeling way too vulnerable and exposed. Not about to let him know that, however, she lifted her chin. "You are making a mountain out of a molehill."

Travis undid his bow tie, leaving the ends to trail on either side of his stiff collar, and opened the first button on his pleated shirt. The overall effect was more devastatingly masculine than ever. "Would you like to know what kind of an evening it was for me?" he asked, studying her.

His quiet, understanding voice sent a shiver down her spine. "Ego building?"

His grin widened even as his brown eyes gentled. "Try excruciating."

Steadying herself by grasping the banister, she slipped off her stiletto heels. The cool terrazzo floor under her stocking feet was wonderfully soothing. Still holding his eyes, she glided closer. "You really didn't seem to be suffering all that much."

Travis undid the second button on his shirt. "In company I can put on a polite smile with the best of them."

Though it was difficult, she continued holding his

steady, assessing gaze. "I heard you laughing." With pleasure. Lots and lots of pleasure.

Travis lifted his broad shoulders in a careless shrug. "Some of what people were saying to me was hilarious. We had a few real comediennes there. But that doesn't mean any of those women interested me the way you do."

Oh, how she wanted to believe that. But the part of her that had been hurt, the part that feared ever being let down in the same way again, was telling her to stop being so reckless and to exercise caution. She came closer still, intending to take him by the hand and show him the door. "In this case, flattery will get you nowhere."

He let her catch his hand, then held his ground and twined his fingers with hers. "What are you really afraid of?"

Chapter Twelve

Travis didn't think Holly was going to answer, at least not candidly. Then she drew a halting breath, looked him straight in the eye and said, "I'm afraid that my relationship with you will end up the same way my relationship with Cliff ended."

Of all the weapons she could have used against him, this hurt the most. Travis clenched his jaw. "That's not fair."

Her lips compressed, she came toward him in a drift of perfume. "In the beginning of my marriage, everything was great—at least on the surface." She lifted her elegant shoulders in a small shrug. "We had fun together, we wanted all the same things—a nice home, satisfying careers, the sense of continuity married people have in each other. In the end, he realized he had many more options than he'd originally thought. He realized he could move from the Texas banking scene to the international."

Travis had an idea where this was going. He shrugged out of his tuxedo jacket and draped it on the coat tree in the hall. "Just like I could move from the girl next door to the oil heiress at the Kimball Museum."

His small gibe was meant to bring Holly back to the reality of their situation. Instead, it only made her sadder, more circumspect.

"That date with you cost the winning bidder *ten thousand dollars,* Travis." Twin spots of color flushed her fair cheeks. "I may not know who the woman was who won the evening with you, but I do know I can't compete with that. I'll never be able to compete with that."

His heart going out to her, Travis went over and put his hands on her shoulders. He knew how it felt to be afraid the passion was too good to be true. He felt that way now. The difference was he wasn't going to let his own uncertainty get in the way of what they could have if only they were brave enough to stay the course. "I'm not asking you to," he said quietly, brushing a strand of hair from her cheek.

Holly shrugged and held his eyes with difficulty. "Maybe not now." Her lower lip quivered. "But you know what they say. One taste of caviar and champagne, and you'll never go back to beer and nachos...."

Travis rubbed his thumb across her lower lip, tracing the softness and the shape. "Anyone who says that doesn't know me," he told her, his voice husky but firm. "I have my own company. I could live in a ten-million-dollar home right now if I wanted."

She studied his face gravely. "But you don't."

He sat down on the edge of the foyer table and tugged her between his spread knees. "It's not my style—and never will be."

Holly sighed, mindlessly fiddling with the buttons on his shirt.

"For me," Travis continued, curving a hand over her silky bare shoulder, "the finer things in life involve love, passion and fun…and marathon baking sessions for the annual preschool cookie swap." He waited until she met his eyes again before he continued with affection, "It's coming over to your house all the time and having you come to mine. It's being with you and all the kids. And being here with you, just the two of us, alone like this," he said, even more softly.

Holly caught her breath. "Travis…"

He looked at her intently. He was not about to play games with something this important or potentially damaging to their relationship, even if it meant she could save face. "I know we said we'd keep this casual," he recalled, the air between them charged with all the things they had left unsaid, up to now. "But casual is not the way I feel."

He lowered his mouth to hers. "Or you, either, if you're honest." He pressed his lips to hers, caressing, learning them anew. "For instance, I know you were thinking about this kiss…wanting it…every time you looked at me tonight…"

Still holding her gently, he ran his tongue along the seam of her lips, until they parted in surrender and she swayed toward him, wanting more.

"And I know," he continued, his voice deepening erotically, "that you like it when I kiss you like this. And you know why?" he whispered fiercely, prepared to be as relentless as he needed to be, in pursuit of her. "Because we belong together, Holly."

For now. For all time…

Holly moaned deep and low in her throat, and then

arched against him and kissed him back with even less restraint than he had shown.

He drew her flush against him, so she could feel his hardness. He wanted her to know how much she excited him, and he wanted to arouse her, too. Passionate longing swept through him as the continued thrust and parry of their tongues sent a wake-up call through every cell of their bodies.

Travis swept her into his arms and headed up the stairs, knowing that when they made love tonight, it was going to be hotter and wilder than anything either of them had ever experienced.

And Holly knew it, too. It was in her eyes when he set her down next to her bed and reached around her to release the zipper on her evening gown. Pulse pounding, senses already in an uproar, he helped her off with the dress. It was going to be a hell of an effort, but this time, he promised himself, he was going to go slow. Make sure she got every ounce of enjoyment out of this, and then some.

She hitched in a breath as he helped her off with her bustier, too, and explored the satiny pink tip of a nipple with the pad of his thumb.

"And there are many things we haven't yet had a chance to do," he murmured, stroking her lovely curves, moving from the rounded globe of one breast to the other, to her long, lissome thighs.

She hitched in a breath as he divested her of her stockings and panties. "I think I'm getting the idea," she murmured breathlessly, unbuttoning his shirt.

He shifted her onto the bed, onto her back. Draping a leg over her thighs, he continued caressing her with the flat of his palm and his fingertips, making his way from her breasts to her collarbone, to her navel, studiously avoiding the part he most wanted to touch. He kissed her all the while, until she made a soft helpless sound that sent his own arousal into overdrive.

Burning with a need he could no longer deny, he guided her to the edge of the bed. He knelt on the floor in front of her and pulled her knees apart. She whimpered in delight as he breathed in the musky scent of her and then leaned forward to caress her damp, petal-soft skin, over and over. Satisfaction unlike anything he had ever known flowed through him when she gasped, gripped his shoulders and came apart in his hands.

His own body thrumming with the need to have her, he held her until the tremors subsided, then stood and divested himself of his clothing.

Holly had known from the first time Travis kissed her that the desire she felt for him was something she couldn't fight. So she had decided rather than try and resist it, she would allow them to have a fling, and when that didn't end as expected, an ongoing physical relationship that went along with their already well-established friendship.

But when he joined her on the bed again, when he let her explore his body as thoroughly as he had learned her own, when he finally could stand it no more and kissed her again with the tenderness and patience and adoration only a dream lover could possess, she knew much more was going on here than she had ever expected.

The impossible was happening. She had fallen head over heels in love with Travis. And those feelings only intensified as he draped her body with his own, slid his hands beneath her hips and lifted her against him. He entered her with excruciating slowness and care, taking command in a thoroughly proprietary male way that aroused her all the more.

Holly cried out softly, tangling her hands in his hair. Moving her palms over his shoulders, down his back, wanting him never to stop. And he didn't. He took control of the mesmerizing pleasure, making it as hot and wanton as the emotions swirling inside her. Pausing and withdrawing, going deeper every time. Until she was arching her back and rocking against him, reveling in the erotic feelings, the sweet hot need, knowing that this time she was his, not just for the moment or the night, but for now and forever.

As GOOD AS THEIR lovemaking was Saturday night, their shopping expedition on Sunday afternoon was even better. To Holly's and Travis's delight, the kids were thrilled with the opportunity to pick out gifts, and couldn't wait to get home and wrap them.

"Daddy, you are never going to guess what's inside this!" Sophie exclaimed as she put her clumsily wrapped gift under the tree in Travis's family room.

"It's not socks!" Mia declared.

Sophie shook her head vigorously. "Nope! It is definitely not socks!"

"It could be a coloring book," Holly prompted with a helpful grin.

"Nope. It's not a coloring book, either!" Sophie said, not getting the hint Holly desperately wanted them to take before they gave everything away.

"It's not a tie, either!" Mia handed Travis her own gift to him.

Tucker passed Travis a flat rectangular box, covered in Snoopy cartoon Christmas paper. "I can't 'member what's inside this," he said with a baffled shrug.

Tristan elbowed his twin. "Our present goes under the tree, not to Travis, " he chided. "And the wallet's not for now! It's for Christmas!"

Travis regarded all the children, deadpan. "I am sure I will be very surprised," he said.

Their excitement nearly overwhelming them, they raced back to the foyer to get the rest of the gifts they had wrapped.

"Mommy, all of these are for you!" Tucker announced as he put a small square box wrapped in silver next to the others under the tree.

Tristan added a slightly smaller box.

"Don't worry." Travis winked. "It's not popcorn or peppermint!"

"And it's not perfume!" Sophie declared as she shook a box vigorously, delighting at the sound of liquid inside, before setting it ever so gently under the tree.

"I'll keep that in mind," Holly said soberly.

Mia added hers to the heap. "And it's not something aqua, like your eyes."

Now that, Holly noted, was interesting.

A scarf, perhaps?

Travis's expression revealed no clue. But he had helped the children pick out the gifts for her, just as she had helped them picked ones for him.

"Don't forget Mrs. Ruley," Travis reminded them.

The children raced back to get those gifts, too. "She's really going to like them," Sophie declared in excitement.

"Yes," Holly said, "she is." The kids had chosen

chocolate candy, English breakfast tea, scones and a sachet in her favorite lavender scent for their nanny.

They plopped down on the floor in front of the tree, admiring their handiwork once again. "Mommy, can we listen to Christmas music before we have supper?" Tucker asked.

She nodded. "That's a very good idea." After a marathon of shopping and wrapping, they all needed a little downtime.

The kids were finally settled. Travis and Holly left them there, still giggling and whispering about their gifts, and retired to the kitchen. "I think this is the first year they all seem to have an idea what's going on," he said.

Holly got out the skillet and handed him a dozen eggs. It was a breakfast-for-dinner evening. While he set about cracking them into a bowl, she added frozen hash brown potatoes to a skillet, and layered slices of turkey bacon on the microwave cooking plate. "I know—they were so cute today. And so serious about picking out their presents."

"I really felt like we were a regular family," he stated.

Holly turned and looked into his eyes. "So did I," she said softly.

Travis's gaze turned unbearably tender. "It was a good feeling."

"A very good feeling," she agreed.

The next thing she knew he had crossed the distance between them, taken her into his arms and was kissing her like it was Christmas. And maybe, Holly thought, kissing him back in exactly the same way, it was.

"I have one more request," Travis said, when at last they drew apart.

She smiled up at him warmly. "And that is?"

"About my proposal that our two families spend the holiday together this year, as one…?"

Holly couldn't think of anywhere she and her boys would rather be but with him and the girls. "Consider it a date."

SUNDAY EVENING CONTINUED TO be magical, as Travis and Holly made plans for exactly how the holiday would play out, right down to what they were going to cook for Christmas dinner, and the time they'd get up on Christmas morning.

On Monday, however, reality hit.

At noon, as previously arranged, Travis accompanied Holly to Martin Shield's office, where Cliff was waiting. Also there, to Holly's surprise, was Simon Armstrong.

Holly hadn't seen Simon in nearly three years. Always on the chunky side, he had gained a little more weight and had gray around his temples. But he was the same exceedingly decent man she remembered. Kind and cordial. Very down-to-earth.

Holly assumed Simon was there for the same reason Travis was, to lend moral support.

Martin Shield waited until everyone was seated, then turned to Holly.

"As you know, at the time of your divorce years ago, Cliff set up trust funds in the boys' names that will cover any and all expenses you might have rearing them, as well as their education, through the college and postgraduate years. The court accepted this lump-sum payment in lieu of monthly child support and an additional trust of alimony for you, because they deemed it in the best fiscal interests of you and the children."

"I appreciated the responsible way this was handled," Holly said quietly. Cliff's generosity had meant she hadn't needed to work at all during the first two years of the twins' lives. She had been able to purchase outright a comfortable home in a nice neighborhood, and when she had gone back to work, she had been able to afford a housecleaning service as well as a nanny.

Martin Shield continued, "He also asked for no visitation, and granted sole custody of the twins to you."

"Over my protests," Holly reminded them. At the time, she had wanted her ex-husband to continue to see the boys, in the vain hope Cliff would come to love them as deeply as she did.

"You know that never would have worked," Cliff interjected, beginning to look a little impatient. "I discovered I'm not the parental type. And frankly, it's not something that can be faked."

He was right about that, Holly thought. Cliff didn't seem to respond to children at all. Whereas someone like Travis loved all kids as much as they loved him.

"Consequently," Martin Shield continued in his deep, officious baritone, "Cliff would like to terminate his parental rights to the boys."

Holly stared at the distinguished attorney, certain she could not have heard correctly. Of all the things she had expected, it wasn't this!

"Unfortunately," he said with a frown, "this is no simple feat in the state of Texas. The courts here require that two parents be responsible for any offspring, whenever possible, and will not permit any one parent

to terminate their responsibility to their offspring—
fiscally or otherwise—unless there is another parent
immediately willing to step in and take on such responsibility through formal adoption. That person must be
approved by the guardian ad litem appointed by the
court to look after the child's interests. When all is in
order, the guardian ad litem report, the termination of
parental right, and the adoption must occur on the same
day, concurrently, as part of one procedure."

"Which is why I'm here," Simon interjected. He looked
Holly in the eye, his manner as genuine and kind as his
voice. "I've always wanted kids. I've known all along
what a treasure you have in those twin boys of yours."

"And he never let me forget it," Cliff said, just as
honestly. "Which is why when I found out that I would
not be able to sever ties with the children without finding
another father for them, I immediately thought of Simon.
He's here in Texas. He's ready and willing to take on the
task of single fatherhood in a way I simply can't."

"Naturally, it wouldn't happen overnight," Simon
said. "I'd start out spending time with the kids, acting
as an 'uncle' figure in their lives, taking them to the zoo
and playing baseball with them, and ultimately being
legally responsible for them without stepping in as a traditional father. We can all agree that would be a little
too presumptuous." Simon paused. "I just want to make
sure the twins have a father figure in their lives."

They already have one, Holly thought. And a very
fine one at that!

"So if you agree," Simon proposed hopefully, direct-
ing Holly's attention back to the crazy plan her ex and
Simon had cooked up.

"Are you nuts?" Holly shot back. She had so many objections to this travesty of an idea she didn't know where to begin.

She glared at the three men who had so thoughtfully arranged this for her, not sure whom to let have it first!

Travis looked equally incensed. But he was a lot quicker to put his thoughts together.

"Hold it right there!" he commanded flatly. He stood, interrupting the proceedings, and he squared off with the other men in the room. "I don't know what you all think you're trying to pull here, but Simon Armstrong is not Holly and the boys' only option!"

HIS PRONOUNCEMENT WAS MET with differing emotions, Travis noted. Martin Shield looked impressed. Simon Armstrong appeared crushed to think his chance to be a dad was curtailed yet again. Cliff Baxter seemed ticked off—probably because he didn't like having his high-handed, thoroughly obnoxious plans derailed. And Holly just looked stunned and brokenhearted. Which in turn broke Travis's heart. The last thing his woman needed was to be disrespected by that cur of an ex-husband again.

"I'm available, if the boys need a father," he declared.

Holly jumped out of her seat. "If they need a father, I'll find them one!" she cried. Looking and sounding more emotional than ever, she turned to Simon first. "If you want to be a single dad so badly I suggest you find children to foster or adopt on your own!" Holly whirled back to Cliff. "How could you do this," she asked angrily. "And at Christmas, no less! *Why* would you do this?" Moisture gleamed in her eyes. "Why did you even want to see them at all if this is what you had planned?"

He lifted an indifferent hand and then let it drop back to his lap. "I asked to see them because I wanted to make sure I didn't have some father-son bond with them, after all. As you probably noted—" he paused to let his words sink in "—I didn't. And I did try to feel something when I saw them, Holly." He searched his ex-wife's eyes. "Some paternal pride, some familial bond, something!"

"But you didn't," Holly noted sadly, in the awkward silence that fell.

"In fact," Travis snarled, finding it hard to curtail his own loathing, "you could barely force yourself to stay and chat with them for half an hour."

"It was torture," Cliff stated, owning up to his feelings honestly.

Tears pooled on Holly's lashes, but did not fall. "I get that you don't want to see them or have much to do with them," she said thickly, her whole body trembling, "but do you have to disown them—as if they're nothing to you?"

Cliff winced. "Actually," he began, exchanging looks with Simon.

"He does if he wants to marry Penelope Kensington," Simon explained, for his friend.

"The famous English doll manufacturer," Holly murmured numbly.

Cliff nodded, looking earnest once again. He leaned forward persuasively. "I love her. She loves me. But she does not want to be stuck bringing up someone else's children, so the only way we'll marry is if I sever ties with the boys."

Holly threw up her hands in disgust. "And who said

you didn't have a heart," she muttered, looking as if it was all she could do not to deck Cliff then and there.

Travis felt the same way, but brawling would solve nothing. They were here in the attorney's office to craft a solution not make matters worse.

"Please do this," Cliff begged Holly. "It's the only way I'll ever get what I want."

"And it's all about you, isn't it?" she asked wearily.

Cliff had no answer for the rhetorical question, but Travis knew that none was required.

"I MEANT WHAT I SAID," Travis told Holly after they left the attorney's office, with nothing resolved save the fact that she refused to make a decision of such importance in the space of a few minutes. She was determined to take as much time as she needed to think about all this.

Travis paused next to his SUV. "If Cliff doesn't want your boys, I do! I love them like my own, Holly. You know that."

She leaned against the passenger door, making no move to open it and get in. "It's not that simple, Travis."

He jingled the keys in his hand. "It can be. We've already talked about marrying—"

Her eyes glittered furiously. "As a convenience, and I vetoed that suggestion."

"You've also vetoed ever falling in love again, or trusting that any romantic relationship would last forever."

"Because," Holly repeated with a soul-deep sigh, "romance is based on an illusion of perfection. And that illusion can't last when confronted with the wear and tear of everyday living."

Travis grasped her arms and held her in front of him.

"But friendship can last under those conditions. And you and I are best friends. We love each other's children as our own and have already agreed to stand in as Mommy and Daddy as needed." Raw emotion filled his voice. "We share every aspect of our daily lives and practically live at each other's houses. And yesterday when we felt like we were one family you were as thrilled as I was."

"And I still am." Holly stood stiffly in his arms.

Stung as much by the look in her eyes as by her words, Travis let her go and stepped back. "But…?"

Holly ran a hand through her hair and continued in a cold, calm voice Travis found much more terrifying than her anger. "Look, I know how competitive you are, how you hate it when the bad guys win, and always want justice to prevail. I know how angry you are about the way Cliff has behaved, and that you want my kids to have all the love they deserve and a father who cherishes them." She sighed. "And I know you want your daughters to have the mommy they want for Christmas, too. But I would never ask you to take on legal responsibility for my kids, any more than you would ask me to do that strictly to make life easier in the moment, Travis."

Was that what this was to her—a moment? Was that all they were? Apparently so, Travis noted, not sure when he had felt more disappointed. He stared at her with a growing sense of disillusionment. "Because that would be permanent, wouldn't it?" And Holly didn't take risks like that. Not anymore, he realized sadly.

She narrowed her eyes, on the defensive once again. "What do you mean—that would be permanent?"

"None of this is about you not trusting romance!" He pointed an accusing finger at her heart. "It's about you not trusting me!"

Holly's jaw dropped. "I do trust you!" she vowed.

Really? Travis folded his arms in front of him, and waited for the truth to come out. "Enough to believe I won't one day do to you what Cliff did…and continues to do?" he challenged, studying the conflicting play of emotions on her face. "The man is a donkey's rear end!" *And I'm being punished for it,* Travis thought, incensed.

"Believe me, I know what a jackass he is! But he is still the kids' father."

Travis shook his head, stubbornly cutting off that line of argument. "Not in any way that counts," he declared.

"Listen to me, Travis, it's bad enough that Cliff has deserted his children!" Holly continued in a choked voice. "But for the twins to find out he's trying to disown them? That will destroy them when they are old enough to understand!"

Travis ignored the hurt and betrayal glimmering in her eyes. He caught her and held her still when she would have run. "If the boys had me in their lives, it wouldn't matter what Cliff did or did not do for them— because they would know that I love them more than life and would be there for them always."

The look on her face told him his words were falling on deaf ears. Travis let her go once again. Stepped back, this time for good. He surveyed Holly with a coldness that rivaled her own, noting the growing aloofness in her eyes. "But you can't trust that I will be there for them, over the long haul, can you, Holly?" he whispered, more hurt and disappointed than he ever had been in his life.

She swallowed, her own insecurity showing. "I think if you adopt them, you'll be there for the kids," she said after a moment.

Well, that was something, Travis noted, not sure whether to be relieved or worried.

Holly was quiet a long time, looking at the ground. When she finally glanced up at him again, the invisible force field was back around her heart, regret and sorrow in her eyes. "It's the two of us I'm worried about. You can pretend all you want, but at the end of the day you are a man who needs love, Travis," she reminded him, concern and selflessness etched in her features. She held up a palm before he could interrupt. "Not the kind we share, but the deeply romantic, enduring kind you had with Diana."

Holly shook her head, looking to be near tears, then continued thickly, "Maybe you don't miss it now. But you will," she insisted stubbornly, stepping back and away from him. "And I don't want to be there when that day comes, and little by little, your feelings for me begin to change." She swallowed as if just the idea of it was more painful than she could bear. "Instead of feeling drawn to me, you'll feel shackled."

He knew she wanted to believe that. He also knew it was an excuse to cover her fear. "I'm not Cliff," he insisted quietly, hoping to be able to bring her to her senses.

"No, you're not," Holly countered evenly. "You're a million times more of a man than he ever will be. And that is why you deserve better than I can ever give you."

Chapter Thirteen

On the morning of Christmas Eve, Travis said goodbye to all four children as they left for a day of yuletide festivities at Mrs. Ruley's home. Fifteen minutes later, he stood outside in the surprisingly bitter wind, watching as a Carson Construction truck parked in front of the house. A pickup and trailer, with a forklift loaded on the back, followed.

Travis showed the two guys who were making the delivery where the "gifts" were to go.

He knew Holly was home.

He half expected her to come out and watch as the playhouse and spaceship were situated in each of their backyards, then draped with black tarps that would obscure them from view until the kids were presented with them the following morning.

She didn't. But then, she hadn't had much to say to him since she had rejected his proposal.

Travis paid the guys well, thanked them for working on Christmas Eve and headed back inside.

Moments later, the doorbell rang.

He hastened to answer it. But instead of the neighbor

he wished to see, Grady's wife, Alexis, stood on the other side of the door. He had only to glance at her face, to see she was in full matchmaker mode.

"I'm really not in the mood for a pep talk," he said, ushering her in.

Alexis slipped off her jacket and hung it on the coat tree in the foyer. "That's too bad," she told him with the resolve of a woman on a mission, as she walked in to admire the presents under the Christmas tree. "Because you really need one."

Dejectedly, Travis followed. He'd never felt less Christmas spirit in his life. "She rejected my proposal. Twice."

Alexis lifted her hand in an elegant gesture. "Ring and all, I suppose."

Guilt flooded his heart. "I didn't have a ring."

She settled comfortably on the sofa. "Then it must have been oh, so romantic."

Travis continued to pace. "Holly isn't a romantic woman."

Alexis shook her head. "All women are romantic, deep down," she told him with a soft smile. "Some of us just don't want to admit it."

Travis met her gaze. "You never had a problem with that."

"Right," she reflected pleasantly. "It was Grady who did. And look what happened."

Travis warmed at the thought of how happy Grady was now that he allowed love to come back into his life. "He came around to your way of thinking," Travis recalled.

Alexis stood and moved gracefully toward him. "I know you feel hurt and angry, but you have to realize that Holly is in a very tough situation."

Travis felt a muscle tick in his jaw. "You think I don't know that?" He paused to clear his throat. "I'm the one who's had to stand around and watch her suffer through her ex's machinations!"

Alexis placed a hand on his arm and kept it there until he met her penetrating gaze. "And now you're making Holly suffer, too," she concluded with the expertise earned from working in the romance arena.

Travis did a double take. "Excuse me?"

Alexis's eyes narrowed. She held her ground and summed up the situation neatly, "It's your way or the highway."

Anger flared within Travis. "She's the one who dumped *me*." He aimed a thumb at his chest.

Alexis's eyes narrowed. She held her ground and summed up the situation neatly. "Your relationship with Holly isn't a competition to be won, Travis. Personal lives are different than business."

"I know that," Travis replied curtly.

"Do you?" Alexis countered. "Because right now it seems to me that your fierce competitive nature, your need to always see the good guys win in the end, is the real problem here."

Anger flared within Travis. He'd be the first to admit he'd fought hard for Holly. She just hadn't wanted to be won. "I think we're getting off the point," he groused. "Holly is the one who dumped *me*." He aimed a thumb at his chest.

"Only after you gave her a proposal no woman in her right mind would have accepted," Alexis countered, with the same love and understanding she showed everyone around her. Quietly, she beseeched, "Had you been willing to give Holly the ultimate gift, and sacrificed your own needs—in the short term—and been *patient...*"

Travis was so tired of waiting! Of having complete happiness just within his reach, only to experience it briefly...and then have it snatched away again. "We've known each other for over two years!" he reminded her.

"Exactly." Alexis nodded, her resolve strengthening. "And in that time Holly has shown you how she felt about you and your daughters day after day...."

Travis couldn't deny that was true. Holly had been there for him and the girls through good times and bad. Always at the ready with a kind gesture or understanding glance. "You're saying I should just continue to be there for her, whenever she needs me."

Alexis shrugged. "Isn't that what you agreed to do for her sons?" She paused, letting her words sink in. "Why not do it for her, too?"

HOLLY WAS UPSTAIRS, TRYING to decide what to do with Travis's Christmas present, when she saw Alexis McCabe's car drive away from Travis's house. Shortly thereafter, Travis left in his SUV. And then another four vehicles parked in front of her house.

She frowned as the occupants got out, strode up her front walk and rang the bell. Not sure she was up to such a dramatic show of concern, Holly put on her game face and opened the door. All four of Travis's best guy friends stood there. All clearly with one thing on their mind. The last thing she needed was them making her feel worse than she already did about the way things had turned out with her and Travis.

Using humor as her primary defense, she angled her

thumb left and drawled, "If you are looking for Travis, I think you want the house next door."

The four merely grinned. "We found the lady we want to see," Grady said, leading the way inside, with the typical McCabe swagger.

No doubt he and his wife were in cahoots about this yuletide matchmaking strategy, Holly thought. The question was, what had Alexis said to Travis? And what were the guys about to say to her?

"We're at the right place," Jack agreed.

Dan carried a gift-wrapped serving plate of amazing looking cookies from the woman he loved, chef Emily Stayton. "Where should I put these?" he asked jovially.

Giving up, Holly directed, "The kitchen." Clearly, Travis's friends weren't leaving until they said what they had to say. Until then she might as well make herself comfortable and hear them out. Who knew, maybe they would be able to help Travis and her both deal with the fallout from their breakup. If it could even be called that, she thought dispiritedly. Was it a breakup if they'd been intimately involved only a few weeks?

Looking as if he'd had another late night on the Fort Worth social scene, Nate looked longingly at the pot of coffee she had just brewed. He clapped a companionable hand on her shoulder. "Any chance I could get a cup?"

Holly rolled her eyes at the group. "Sit down." She waved a hand at the kitchen table, unwrapped the platter of cookies and put it on the center. Poured everyone, including herself, a cup of coffee, then sat down with them. "Obviously, you've heard that Travis and I went down a road we never should have traveled."

"Or in other words," Grady interjected with his customary bluntness, "you broke Travis's heart."

"No." Holly made a face at them, then explained, "I broke up with him so I *wouldn't* break his heart."

"Try telling him that," Dan muttered with a worried frown. He leaned toward her urgently. "Seriously, Holly, I've known the guy for years and I've never seen him so blue."

"And at Christmas, yet," Jack lamented.

Okay, Holly did feel guilty about that. Especially since she and Travis had made all these plans to spend Christmas together this year. And now it just felt awkward. To the point they had stopped talking, and instead were communicating only as absolutely necessary, through their shared nanny. Yet as much as it hurt her to not have Travis in her life right now, she had to be practical here and do what was best for everyone, not just what would make her happy in the short run. "Look, guys, what Travis offered to do for me was very gallant, and I appreciate his chivalry, but I can't let him adopt my children and marry me just to let my exhusband off the hook!"

"Of course you can't!" Grady concurred, with a grim, disapproving look. "That lousy excuse for a dad doesn't deserve special accommodation from you— or Travis!"

Dan, who knew a thing or two about errant exspouses who hurt their kids with their noninvolvement, harrumphed. "Cliff should have known that in cases like this it's always better to lie to kids, and pretend you care, even when you don't."

He had a point, Holly realized.

"Have you given your ex an answer to his request to terminate his parental rights?" Jack asked, more gently now.

Holly shook her head. "But maybe," she said slowly, as the long-term implications of Travis's offer—and her refusal—sank in, "it's time I did."

TRAVIS WAS JUST RETURNING from the mall, and some last minute Christmas shopping, when he saw his four best friends driving away from Holly's house. Swearing—because this was something else that had not been in his plans—Travis pocketed the gift he'd just purchased and headed across the lawn to Holly's front porch.

She answered the door on the first ring. He held up a silencing palm. "I don't know what was going on just now, but I didn't send them over here."

Holly smiled, looking more peaceful than he had seen her in days. "I know. I didn't imagine you asked Alexis to come by this morning, either."

Travis thought about the heart-to-heart conversation that had set him straight. "You saw her?"

"Oh, yeah." Holly's soft lips twisted into a rueful grin. "It's kind of hard to miss when Foreverlove.com's premiere matchmaker shows up at your love's door."

Travis paused, sure he couldn't have heard right. "You want to back up here a moment and explain?"

The aura of serenity around Holly increased. "Yes. But first I need to make two calls." Graceful and feminine as ever, she ushered him inside. "Can you wait?"

Travis nodded and Holly disappeared into her home office. When she came out, she looked very much at peace…and very besotted with him. As if she wanted them to pick up where they'd left off before the breakup.

Wordlessly, she took him by the hand. When they were settled comfortably on the sofa, she tightened her grasp. "We need to talk…and I want to go first," she insisted, a telltale sheen in her eyes.

Travis inhaled deeply and looked down at their entwined fingers. He let his breath out slowly as the first glimmer of hope rose inside his chest. "Okay."

Holly smiled at him with all the joy he had ever wanted to see on her beautiful face, and gazed deep into his eyes. "I'm taking you up on the offer to adopt the kids. I want to help Cliff terminate his parental rights."

Travis savored the warmth of her slender frame, snuggled next to his. "You were pretty opposed to this the other day," he reminded her in a rusty-sounding voice.

"Only because I was looking at it as a negative instead of a positive," Holly said, holding on to him as if she never wanted to let him go. "The truth is, Cliff hasn't been there for them, not ever. And he doesn't plan to be in the future. Initially, I saw his admission as a blow to the heart. Now I realize that Cliff's brutal honesty and his efforts to help them move on are actually a tremendous sacrifice," she continued in a low, tremulous voice. "And that's how I will explain it to the kids—that some men are not cut out to be daddies. And other men—like you—are, because they have a boundless capacity to love and nurture."

She had taken a situation that could have left her and her sons bitterly disappointed for the rest of their lives, and instead chosen to view it as a rare and special gift of selfless love. Travis's admiration for Holly grew.

"You have the same deeply parental traits," he told her solemnly, admiring her innate ability to comfort, appreciate and bring out the best in those around her.

"Which is why I would like to adopt your little girls, too. I know we didn't get that far in the discussion the other day, but it only seems fair. And, most importantly, it's what I want because I love them, too, Travis, so very much, and I do consider them my own."

With the family he had wanted now becoming a reality, Travis's heart swelled with the happiness she clearly shared. Pulse pounding, he shifted her onto his lap. "What about us?" he asked her huskily.

The hesitation he expected to see was gone. "I'd still like us to spend Christmas together, as a family." She paused. "As for the two of us—"

"We still have a lot to work out," Travis agreed, "starting with my apology. Because you were right. Cliff's reappearance in your life sent the competitive part of me into overdrive, primarily because I couldn't stand the thought of losing you." Travis's voice caught. It was a moment before he could go on with anything akin to cool. "I realize that I moved too fast to make you mine, that I said and did things that were unwarranted in my efforts to protect you and the kids."

"I made mistakes, too," Holly admitted sincerely. "I let my fear of getting hurt again hinder our relationship."

"But in the end it didn't matter," Travis said.

"Because we came together anyway," Holly agreed with a sigh of contentment.

Only part of the way, Travis thought, aware he still wanted and needed more out of their relationship, and he thought she did, too. He paused and looked deep into her eyes, determined to do whatever it took to finally make this right. "But worst of all, I waited to tell you how I really felt because I didn't want to make you uncomfortable. That doesn't mean I haven't felt it. I love you, Holly," Travis told her hoarsely, "as a friend and a lover, but most essentially, as the woman I want to spend the rest of my life with."

Holly blinked. Her eyes were full of tears. "Oh, Travis, I love you, too!"

Their lips met in a sweet and tender kiss that spoke more about their feelings than words ever could. Contentment filled Travis's heart. This was turning into one incredible Christmas. Or at least it would be if...

He kissed her again, then drew back and asked, "Enough to marry me?" Loving the way she felt in his arms, he held her closer still. "Not as an act of convenience, but for real?"

"Most definitely, for real," Holly cried, clinging to him as if she never wanted to let him go. "And as soon as possible."

Wondering how he had ever managed without her, glad he never would have to again, he withdrew the velvet box in his pocket, extracted the diamond engagement ring and slid it onto her left hand. The tears she'd been holding back spilled down her cheeks as she looked at the sparkling ring.

"How about New Year's Eve?" Travis asked.

Holly started to answer, then paused, clearly confused. "Don't you have a date?"

Travis reached into his pocket and pulled out his second gift for her, the silent auction envelope with the winning number. "I wasn't allowed to place bids," he said. "But my friends had no such restriction. So they worked very hard that evening to make sure I spent New Year's Eve with you."

Only now, a stunned and elated Holly realized, instead of a dream date, they'd have a dream wedding.

Epilogue

Seven days later...

Travis and Holly were stealing a preceremony moment alone when they heard Sophie explain, "So since Santa couldn't bring a mommy this year, he brought us a wedding instead!"

Travis chuckled and pressed a palm to his forehead. Holly laughed, too, as from the other side of the wall, they heard the convoluted explanation continue to an even more outlandish ending. Finally, Travis said, "Do you think she'll ever understand?"

Holly smiled and straightened his tie. "Eventually, all of them will, but for now it's kind of cute."

"Almost as cute as you," Travis murmured, taking in her appearance with another sweeping glance.

They had elected to get married in her home and have the reception in his. All of their loved ones were in attendance, including Travis's buddies as well as a few of Holly's close friends and their families.

Travis was wearing a charcoal-gray suit. Holly had on a fitted white satin suit. In keeping with the holiday, they had left their Christmas trees and all the decorations up, and as a special treat for the kids, had even decorated their playhouse and spaceship with outdoor lights.

But most importantly, at the kids' insistence, there were sprigs of mistletoe everywhere—in every corner of both homes, in Holly's hair, on Travis's lapel and even in the flower baskets the girls were carrying.

Mistletoe, the kids had declared, was responsible for all the love in the air.

For once, Holly couldn't disagree.

She did love Travis. And he loved her. And now that she had finally admitted it, life was looking up indeed.

"Mommy…Daddy—it's time!" Sophie declared, jumping up and down with excitement.

Tucker rushed in, carrying one velvet pillow bearing rings. "Grady says you better get a move on!"

"Nate says it's time to get the party started!" his twin declared.

Alexis swept in, looking radiant. She bent to help the girls straighten the flower baskets looped over their arms. "The minister is waiting."

Travis offered his elbow and Holly took it.

Just off the foyer, the music started.

Everyone rushed to be seated.

The children led the way, sweetly earnest as they fulfilled their duties. Then finally it was Travis and Holly standing next to the glittering Christmas tree, celebrating the holiday, the New Year and their life together.

"We are gathered here together," the minister began. *"…to love and to cherish…from this day forward…"*

"What God has joined together, let no man put

asunder," he concluded. "Travis, you may kiss your bride."

Travis took Holly in his arms. Tears of happiness streamed down her face, to mingle with his. A resounding cheer went up when their lips met.

And then their new life began.

* * * * *

There are two single men left in
THE LONE STAR DADS CLUB.
Watch for Jack's story,
WANTED: ONE MOMMY
coming March 2010,
only from Harlequin American Romance.

*Bestselling author Lynne Graham is back
with a fabulous new trilogy!*

PREGNANT BRIDES

Three ordinary girls—naive, but also honest and plucky…

*Three fabulously wealthy, impossibly handsome
and very ruthless men…*

*When opposites attract and passion leads to pregnancy…
it can only mean marriage!*

*Available next month from Harlequin Presents®:
the first installment*

DESERT PRINCE, BRIDE OF INNOCENCE

* * *

'THIS EVENING I'm flying to New York for two weeks,'
Jasim imparted with a casualness that made her heart sink
like a stone. 'That's why I had you brought here. I own this
apartment and you'll be comfortable here while I'm abroad.'

'I can afford my own accommodation although I may not
need it for long. I'll have another job by the time you
get back—'

Jasim released a slightly harsh laugh. 'There's no need for
you to look for another position. How would I ever see you?
Don't you understand what I'm offering you?'

Elinor stood very still. 'No, I must be incredibly thick
because I haven't quite worked out yet what you're offering
me.…'

His charismatic smile slashed his lean dark visage.
'Naturally, I want to take care of you.…'

HPEX0110A

'No, thanks.' Elinor forced a smile and mentally willed him not to demean her with some sordid proposition. 'The only man who will ever take *care* of me with my agreement will be my husband. I'm willing to wait for you to come back but I'm not willing to be kept by you. I'm a very independent woman and what I give, I give freely.'

Jasim frowned. 'You make it all sound so serious.'

'What happened between us last night left pure chaos in its wake. Right now, I don't know whether I'm on my head or my heels. I'll stay for a while because I have nowhere else to go in the short term. So maybe it's good that you'll be away for a while.'

Jasim pulled out his wallet to extract a card. 'My private number,' he told her, presenting her with it as though it was a precious gift, which indeed it was. Many women would have done just about anything to gain access to that direct hotline to him, but his staff guarded his privacy with scrupulous care.

Before he could close the wallet, his blood ran cold in his veins. How could he have made such a serious oversight? What if he had got her pregnant? He knew that an unplanned pregnancy would engulf his life like an avalanche, crush his freedom and suffocate him. He barely stilled a shudder at the threat of such an outcome and thought how ironic it was that what his older brother had longed and prayed for to secure the line to the throne should strike Jasim as an absolute disaster….

* * *

What will proud Prince Jasim do if Elinor is expecting his royal baby? Perhaps an arranged marriage is the only solution! But will Elinor agree? Find out in DESERT PRINCE, BRIDE OF INNOCENCE by Lynne Graham [#2884], available from Harlequin Presents® in January 2010.

Bestselling Harlequin Presents author

Lynne Graham

brings you an exciting new miniseries:

PREGNANT BRIDES

Inexperienced and expecting, they're forced to marry

Collect them all:

DESERT PRINCE, BRIDE OF INNOCENCE

January 2010

RUTHLESS MAGNATE, CONVENIENT WIFE

February 2010

GREEK TYCOON, INEXPERIENCED MISTRESS

March 2010

New Year, New Man!

For the perfect New Year's punch,
blend the following:

- *One woman determined to find her inner vixen*
- *A notorious—and notoriously hot!—playboy*
- *A provocative New Year's Eve bash*
- *An impulsive kiss that leads to a night of*
  explosive passion!

When the clock hits midnight Claire Daniels
kisses the guy standing closest to her, but
the kiss doesn't end after the bells stop ringing....

Look for

Moonstruck

by *USA TODAY* bestselling author

JULIE KENNER

Available January

red-hot reads

www.eHarlequin.com

HB79518

REQUEST YOUR FREE BOOKS!

2 FREE NOVELS PLUS 2 FREE GIFTS!

HARLEQUIN®

American Romance®

Love, Home & Happiness!

YES! Please send me 2 FREE Harlequin® American Romance® novels and my 2 FREE gifts (gifts are worth about $10). After receiving them, if I don't wish to receive any more books, I can return the shipping statement marked "cancel." If I don't cancel, I will receive 4 brand-new novels every month and be billed just $4.24 per book in the U.S. or $4.99 per book in Canada.* That's a savings of close to 15% off the cover price! It's quite a bargain! Shipping and handling is just 50¢ per book. I understand that accepting the 2 free books and gifts places me under no obligation to buy anything. I can always return a shipment and cancel at any time. Even if I never buy another book from Harlequin, the two free books and gifts are mine to keep forever.

154 HDN E4DS   354 HDN E4D4

Name _____ (PLEASE PRINT) _____

Address _____ Apt. # _____

City _____ State/Prov. _____ Zip/Postal Code _____

Signature (if under 18, a parent or guardian must sign)

Mail to the **Harlequin Reader Service:**
IN U.S.A.: P.O. Box 1867, Buffalo, NY 14240-1867
IN CANADA: P.O. Box 609, Fort Erie, Ontario L2A 5X3

Not valid to current subscribers of Harlequin® American Romance® books.

Want to try two free books from another line?
Call 1-800-873-8635 or visit www.morefreebooks.com.

* Terms and prices subject to change without notice. Prices do not include applicable taxes. N.Y. residents add applicable sales tax. Canadian residents will be charged applicable provincial taxes and GST. Offer not valid in Quebec. This offer is limited to one order per household. All orders subject to approval. Credit or debit balances in a customer's account(s) may be offset by any other outstanding balance owed by or to the customer. Please allow 4 to 6 weeks for delivery. Offer available while quantities last.

Your Privacy: Harlequin is committed to protecting your privacy. Our Privacy Policy is available online at www.eHarlequin.com or upon request from the Reader Service. From time to time we make our lists of customers available to reputable third parties who may have a product or service of interest to you. If you would prefer we not share your name and address, please check here. ☐

HAR09R2